FOR THE

LOVE OF

GINGERBREAD

A Hudson Valley Holiday Romance

Courtney Giardina

Dedication

This book is dedicated to everyone that holds their hometown close to their heart. Don't ever be afraid to return home to find the person you may have lost along the way.

1

Addie

I remember the day I graduated from college. I was gripping tight to my diploma while the big city flashed before my eyes. I pictured myself strolling out of my apartment in Greenwich Village and grabbing a cup of coffee to enjoy in Washington Square Park. Then, I'd hop the E train to Times Square where my job as a web designer for an iconic fashion brand would be waiting for me. It was a good dream; one that came to be thanks to Carrie Bradshaw and multiple Sex and the City marathons that I had watched during my teenage years in my old Victorian in upstate New York.

It had been a few years since graduation day and well, my current life situation didn't look quite like my dreams. I was working in New York City though. I was the personal assistant for the CEO of a new fashion brand. Most of my days were the same. I was sitting at my desk organizing my daily tasks when my boss snuck up from behind me.

"Hey A, what's my schedule look like today?"

I shuffled around the papers that were piled high on my desk until my hand grazed the mouse next to my keyboard. With one click Bill's schedule was in front of me.

"You've got a call at eleven, a lunch meeting at one, and a meeting in the boardroom at three. I'm sending over all the details to you now." I hit the send button and waited for his phone to beep.

"Wonderful. Thank you."

"You're welcome, sir. Oh, and your coffee is on your desk. Two creams, one sugar and splash of vanilla."

"Don't know what I'd do without you. Thanks, A." He squeezed my shoulder before heading back up the stairs to his private office.

I hated being called A. It was a name I let slide only when my dad called me it, but it had seemed impossible since the day I started my assistant job here at this fashion startup for Bill to remember my real name. No matter how many times I would correct him, Adelynne would always become Madison or Madeline, and a few random times he called me Addison. It was close. I'd give him that, but I folded after the first year. *"Just called me A,"* I told him. So far, he hasn't messed that up. I didn't think I'd still be here two years later for it to matter so much, but here I was, another year coming to an end and my feet were still permanently planted on the ground in front of the corporate ladder.

Once Bill had retreated into his office, I went back to the long list on the computer in front of me. I had to pick up the newest line from the dry cleaners and set them up in the studio so it would be ready for the big New Year's photoshoot. I still had a few flights to book for models that would be coming up and I had to stop at the restaurant where Bill was taking his friends to dinner on Christmas Day. The menu still needed to be finalized and well... that fell under my job description.

Time was of the essence today because I was heading back home to Cold Spring in the morning for holiday break. Christmas was next week and my sister had guilted me into coming home this year. It would be the first Christmas in three years I'd be going home. The last two years, I pretended that my deadlines were tight. *Fashion never sleeps,* I told my mom. She didn't object, but even with the dismal tone in her voice, she understood, and I needed that.

Instead of sitting in the office working on deadlines, I spent Christmas alone with a small, fake tree sitting atop the only table that could fit inside my three hundred square foot apartment in Queens. When Mom called me on Christmas morning, I'd open up the window and let the typical sounds of the city in. *"I'm on my way into the office,"* I'd say. The never-ending sound of car horns escaping through the window made it believable over the phone.

I probably would've done the same thing this year if I didn't have a new nephew to meet. His name was Dylan and he was two months old. I was reminded of his adorable blond head of hair every time I opened my phone. On my screensaver, he was dressed in the yellow duck onesie I had sent home for the baby shower. His eyes were closed and one hand rested snug by his ear. I was so focused on Dylan that I didn't notice the shadow creeping across my desk.

"What time are you heading out tomorrow?"

I jerked my head up at the same time my phone slammed onto the desk. My coworker Brody was sitting comfortable on my desk with his arms crossed. He looked so proper in his maroon button up and khaki pants.

It was hard not to envy Brody. He was a design assistant for the company's summer line. I had applied for his job when I first saw it pop up on the website, but he had more experience coming from a fitness apparel line just down 7th street. He was a couple of years older than I was. In our spare time, he turned me on to a new passion of mine - photography. We'd go to Central Park and he'd show me how to work the camera and the best angles to capture images. I was a better photographer because of him and possibly a more well-rounded local foodie as well.

"I think I'm going to try and catch the 10:45 a.m. out of Grand Central," I answered.

"Nice! Does today's workload allow you to sneak away for some lunch?"

I looked at the computer screen and knew my answer should have been no, but the rumble that suddenly emerged from my stomach confirmed it was time to take a break.

"Yes, I think I can," I said. I reached into the oversized bag that rested at my feet for everything that would keep the December air from seeping through to my skin. I wrapped my blue scarf around my neck and slipped on my gloves as Brody opened up the door. Winter in New York City was nothing like where I grew up. I was still getting used to how much of a difference fifty miles could make.

In Cold Spring when it snowed, you would hear shovels along the pavement as people scraped their driveways and snowplows slushing through the streets, but there was something magical about what they left behind. We went about our day with a blanket of white surrounding us. Here in New York, they had to get rid of snow as soon as it fell. It was the only way to keep traffic moving. As Brody and I walked along the sidewalks of SoHo there were no remnants of the fluffy flakes that were falling outside my window the night before.

"How are you feeling?" Brody asked. "About going home?"

I shrugged. Though he didn't know the whole story, Brody had an inkling that I'd been avoiding my hometown for some time now. Every time I'd mentioned in it our conversations a sense of dread filled my voice.

"I'm excited to hold my nephew and I do miss my family. I guess my return was inevitable."

"Yeah. I think it'll be good for you. Are you bringing the rascal? By rascal, Brody meant my seventeen-pound pillow stealer. Hudson was a chocolate-colored ball of fluff that I'd rescued about six months ago. He's mostly mutt, but his floppy ears and soft coat have me believing there's some golden retriever in him.

"I sure am!" I said. "Can't go anywhere without him."

Brody laughed. "Don't I know it. So, are you thinking tacos or the deli?"

I shifted my scarf so that it was now covering my face. The wind was biting hard at my pale skin. "Definitely deli." Tacos were my first choice, but the deli was closer, and I knew I needed to get to the dry cleaners sooner rather than later.

We stepped into the street and glided across the sheets of black ice that covered the crosswalk. The deli was busy, so we got our orders to go and headed back.

Brody pulled open the door to the office and I relished the immediate warmth that hit my cheeks. I unzipped my coat and shook the wetness off before tucking it back into the cubby.

"Thanks for lunch. You didn't have to," I said. I settled in my chair and pulled the cheesesteak sub from the paper bag. Brody never let me pay for anything. It never stopped me from trying, but I failed miserably every time.

"You're welcome. Come here." I stood up and folded myself in his arms. "Have fun at home and Merry Christmas if I don't see you before you go."

"Merry Christmas," I said. I waved to him as he headed up the stairs to where all the non-entry level workers sat. My eyes looked back at the long list still staring at me through the computer. I sat back down and in between each bite of my cheesesteak, I slid the curser down the computer screen, knowing that list was the only thing separating me from facing everything I could no longer avoid.

2

Drake

"Order up!" I hit the bell and slid the plate of today's special onto the front counter. I still can't believe how far this place has come since I first started. The ad was so small I almost missed it. It was in the bottom right corner of the daily newspaper I happened to be flipping through in my parent's living room. I was old school. I loved searching the want ads in black and white instead of scrolling on a computer screen. There was barely any description of what the job entailed, yet somehow that intrigued me.

Help Needed. Café growing. Looking for a new chef with unique menu ideas. Stop in any weekday between noon and two if interested.

Growing up on the opposite side of the river didn't make me a huge expert on the town of Cold Spring, but I had been there a time or two. The last time was maybe ten years ago with my eighth-grade class to dive into the history of the West Point Foundry. I remember stopping at a pizza place on the main strip before the bus took us back over the Newburg-Beacon Bridge for home.

I read the ad four times before I circled it in red and then looked at my watch. I was twenty-three, out of school, and barely making ends meet. I had time to make the forty-minute drive that would eventually lead me to where I was right now, standing in front of the double oven of Mave's Coffeehouse.

"Thanks, Drake," Mave said. She snatched the plate from the counter. Her hair was frazzled from the constant back and forth to the tables that morning. Her white apron had coffee stains on it. Her almond-shaped eyes looked tired and she was out of breath, but there was still a smile on her face seeing how busy we were. It was a rarity these days, so even though I was moving double time, I appreciated it. Mave did too. I looked up to see her peering through the opening that separated the kitchen from the rest of the café. "We're getting low on muffins out here. Do we have any more in there?" Mave asked.

"I think I have one tray. I'll go look." I spun around and hurled myself back towards the pan rack where I found a dozen more blueberry muffins topped with a lemon glaze. I slid them from their place under the double chocolate brownies and restacked the display before taking another ticket from the order line. Mave and I did a little line dancing around each other. There wasn't much room behind the counter and I wasn't sure with her lightning speed through the room that she saw the muffins. "Blueberry muffins are good to go, Mave."

"You're the best decision I ever made." She winked at me.

Mave said I was the best person for the job when she called to offer it to me, but to be honest, I think I was the only one in the running. Growing up in a small town usually means aching for life in a big city, which is where most of those I graduated with ended up. Not me though. I loved being able to see the stars at night. I never needed an alarm clock to wake me up in the morning. The birds did that. The sounds of them chirping their way into my dreams and easing me into the morning light was soothing. I felt the same way about the bell to the café that meant the last customer left for the day.

Don't get me wrong. I love my job, but after a full shift, there's no better feeling than throwing down the towel and letting out a heavy sigh to catch my breath. Mave met me in the kitchen to do the same.

"Today was a good day," she said. "I feel like things are starting to look up." I wrapped my flour-covered arm around her shoulder.

"We'll get there Mave. Business has already started to pick up since we introduced the breakfast menu and baked goods. It's almost doubled our revenue."

The way Mave was staring into the abyss in front of us made me feel sad. The coffeehouse was her late father's legacy. Being an only child, it was both a blessing and a curse when she inherited it. Her memories were alive and well between these walls, but the financials were a mess. She couldn't believe how much her father hadn't told her, but she understood. Second to Mave, the coffeehouse was his baby. He put his heart, soul, and every dollar he ever owned into this place.

"Hopefully we can keep it up," Mave said, "or come the new year we might both be out of a job."

I couldn't stand the thought of not waking up every morning to come to Mave's. Besides my cozy two-bedroom apartment above the hardware store, this is where I spent most of my time. Even after the doors were locked, Mave let me stay and play in the kitchen to see what kind of creation I could come up with next. I liked that a part of me was slowly become immersed here. Before I started, the coffeehouse was strictly that...coffee. There was hot coffee, iced coffee, and blended coffee. After three years of grinding coffee beans without her father, Mave knew she needed to make a change, and thank goodness I needed one too because the two of us made a darn good team.

Mave manned the counter. She made the coffee and served the tables and I tucked myself between the oven and the chopping block to meet the demands of the newly introduced menu I incorporated. When it was really busy, Mave's daughter Alice would help out for a few hours, but being a teenager, working at her mom's place wasn't the cool thing to do.

"Alright kid," Mave said. She pulled the towel slung over her shoulder and whipped it at me. "Get outta here. Go enjoy the day. I'll see you in the morning."

"Are you sure?" I asked. I could tell by the way her brows melted together though that she needed some time alone.

"I'm sure."

"I'll see you tomorrow," I said. I saw my reflection in the metal of the pot hanging above me. My arm wasn't the only thing covered in flour. I dusted the bits of white off my cheeks and my forehead and switched out my chef coat for the winter one hanging by the door.

The sun was hiding today and the snow was falling. It was my favorite kind of snow. The fluffy kind where the snowflakes fall like feathers before they land. I didn't have far to walk back to my place, but the thick blanket of white made it hard to see too far in front of me. Every few feet I'd take a step and the ice would get me. I'd skate my way forward until I caught my balance and I'd start walking again.

I loved the snow. I loved this town. I loved the people. They loved this town and they loved Mave's Coffeehouse. I thought about how long the roots of that coffeehouse were as I pushed through the blindness to the door that would lead me up a flight of stairs to my apartment. I wanted to preserve those roots. Mave's still had a lot more life left in it and I was determined to figure out how to find it.

3

Addie

It was far past rush hour when I walked into Grand Central Terminal, but that didn't matter here. The foot traffic in Midtown Manhattan's elegant landmark never stopped. Hudson trotted along beside me as voices echoed off the tall marble walls that surrounded us. I juggled Hudson's leash, my camera, and suitcase as I dodged those passing me in all directions. I pulled my ticket from the machine and walked over to the track that read Poughkeepsie.

The train was waiting underneath the archway. I could feel my heart rate quicken when I stepped from the platform onto the train. It had been so long since I'd been home. There was no turning back now as I slid into the window seat and lifted Hudson onto my lap. He squirmed in my grasp and placed his front paws on the window ledge. I pulled off my gloves and sent a group text to my mom and my sister.

On train now. See you soon. xoxo

I could picture both of them letting out a heavy sigh of relief once it came through. My mother would then throw her head back, fold her hands in front of her chest, and thank God. Last year she had almost convinced me to make the trip. I had a duffle bag all packed and set on the twin size bed in my apartment the morning before Christmas Eve, but I couldn't bring myself to do it. I think a part of her worried that this year I may do the same.

She replied with a heart emoji and my sister sent a photo of Dylan captioned with the words, *Can't wait to meet my Aunt Addie.* My dad's nickname for me might have been A, but the rest of the world called me Addie. That's how I was known to everyone in my family and everyone in the town of Cold Spring. Everyone in the town of Cold Spring was pretty much family so, it made sense. I liked being called Addie. I also loved that my dad had a special nickname for me, but being called A had its drawbacks. When the bustle of New York City tourists would come into our small town for their weekend getaways, they'd always shout back and forth to their friends when they got separated. In those moments A sounded a lot like "hey." I'd come home most weekends with whiplash after being in town.

I smiled at the photo of Dylan's chubby cheeks. His blue eyes were open wide and I think I even spotted a few blonde hairs on his usually bald head. "Aunt Addie is excited to meet you too," I whispered. The train was relatively quiet. I had the row to myself. My suitcase was nestled in next to me. My camera sat on top of it. The bell rang. My watch read exactly 10:45 a.m. as the train crept slowly out of the station. The darkness of the tunnel was replaced with the bright sunshine of a cold New York day. It beat in through the window as I said goodbye to the tall, tightly packed buildings of the city and hello to the scenic view of the Hudson River.

The first stop was Tarrytown. Hudson had enough of the scenery by then. He pulled his now cold nose from the window and curled up in my lap. I fell asleep sometime before Ossining and I didn't wake until the call for Garrison station came over the speakers. Four minutes, that was how much time I had to gather up my things and my nerves before the train would be pulling into Cold Spring station. If you've never ridden on the Hudson line from New

York City, there's one thing you should know before do. The train, for the most part, runs like clockwork. They're in and out of each station pretty quickly. So, I made sure I was ready when the doors open. Hudson hopped out first. I followed behind him and headed down the stairs to the parking lot where I knew my mom and sister, Victoria, would be waiting.

There wasn't even time to scour the parking lot to find them. As soon as my tan, swede boot hit the snow-covered pavement, I heard a high-pitched scream. My head jolted over in its direction to find them both frantically waving over at me. My cheeks flushed. I waved back. Dylan was covered in an oversized blue snowsuit. His monkey hat was so big on him that he squirmed to remove it from over his eyes. I could hear his faint wince as I walked closer.

"Oh Addie, I'm so glad you're home!" I leaned in and my mom wrapped her arms around me. I tried to keep Hudson's wet paws from landing on her jeans as he jumped to be part of the action. I could feel her firm grip through the puffiness of my jacket. I squeezed back. Immediately I felt a sense of calm wash over me. I'd been avoiding all the feelings that Cold Spring held for two years, thinking that when I returned it would be sadness, not calm that would suffocate me. Standing in that parking lot with the chill of the breeze from the river blowing between us, I felt more home at that moment than I think I ever had.

"And who is this?" Mom bent down to scratch Hudson's ears."

"This is Hudson! They say he's about three years old."

"Wow, so he's fully grown then. What a cute little guy." Mom stood back up and hugged me one more time. "I've missed you so much."

"I missed you too, Mom," I said.

"What about me?" Victoria pulled me toward her. One hand wrapped around me and pulled me in close enough that I was now inches from Dylan's covered eyes.

"I missed you too, of course!" I said. I maneuvered my wool gloves underneath the tip of Dylan's hat and nudged it up so I could see his precious blue eyes. "Well, hello little man. I'm you're Auntie Addie." I brushed my glove covered fingers across his cheek. His angst had turned to contentment and he smiled up at me.

"I can't wait for you to see all he's been doing lately. He's smiling and trying hard to hold his head up. He loves bath time too. I saved his bath for tonight, so you could see."

"Great!"

Dylan's hat fell back down over his eyes. I felt a tug from my shoulder. Mom was steeling my duffle bag to put in the trunk. I pulled open the back door of her SUV and slid in next to the car seat. Victoria pulled Dylan out of his bulky snowsuit and buckled him in next to me.

We didn't have far to go. Two miles and we'd be pulling up alongside our family home, which coincidentally also happened to be the family business. The Church Street Bed & Breakfast opened the year before I was born. With seven bedrooms and four bathrooms, it was the perfect place to call home for all twenty years of my adolescence. When we pulled up in front of it that afternoon, the house was much different than I had remembered.

"You painted the front!" The large bay windows were now surrounded by a greyish blue color and the wrap around porch was highlighted by bright white railings. It was a far cry from the green and black paint that had been slowly chipping off since I was in middle school.

"We did. This past summer," Mom said. "Your father always wanted to paint those railings white."

I laughed. "He sure did." Mom was always against it. She wanted to preserve the history of the bed and breakfast that she'd bought from my grandparents all those years ago. She'd saved every penny she earned from the time she was in college. That's where she met my dad. Born and raised in the hustle and bustle of Manhattan, I don't think he ever saw himself moving to the small town of Cold Spring after the two of them both graduated from Fordham University, but when I was younger he'd always tell me that he never thought twice. His big-city dreams dissipated once he met my mother.

I would've followed her anywhere, he would say, and that he did.

They settled into an apartment in Fishkill once they first moved upstate. Dad took a job at a financial services firm while my mom drove across the river each morning to manage a historical inn.

By the time I came around they were homeowners in Beacon, but when my grandfather fell ill, my grandmother knew the time had come. The seven-bedroom house was too much for her, so they moved into a smaller home a few blocks down and my parents put their first house up for sale and made the big move into business ownership. Less than a year later the bed and breakfast was officially open to visitors.

"I repurposed those Adirondack chairs." Victoria pointed at the cherry wood chairs that lined the front porch.

"They look amazing!" I said. I swung my bag up over my shoulder and slammed the car door behind me. The salt crunched below my feet as I walked down the sidewalk. The door leading inside was an antique. It had been sanded and stained multiple times over the years, but the beauty hadn't faded. A welcome sign hung from a hook beside it. I stepped back to get a better look. The once outdated yet love-filled home I remembered had been rebirthed. My hand slowly unzipped the case that held my camera and I pulled it out. I snapped a photo of the entrance then turned for a panoramic view of the line of Adirondack chairs. I stood on the front porch for a little. Mom and Victoria hung back on the sidewalk. I turned to them and they both smiled at me. With a long, deep inhale I turned the doorknob and stepped inside.

I let go of Hudson's leash and he took off to explore in one direction while I looked around in the other. The inside was almost unrecognizable. The front desk now had a stone surround with the same cherry wood on the counter as the chairs outside. The faded carpet had been replaced with hardwood and the once maroon covered walls were now hidden with beige.

"Hey, Sue!" I waved. Sue has been working at the bed and breakfast for more than a decade. She came out of retirement to lend a hand until things were up and running, but she decided she loved it so much, she wanted to stay.

"Welcome home Addie!" Sue jetted from behind the desk to give me one of her bear hugs. She patted my head and squeezed me so tight my chest barely had room to rise. "It's so good to see you, sweet girl."

"You too! I can't believe how much everything has changed around here. Suddenly I'm a stranger in my own house."

"You've been gone for almost three years, Addie." Victoria swung her arm over my shoulder." There's a lot that can happen in three years."

Three years. It hadn't seemed like I'd avoided this town for that long. I'd graduated from college the summer before I spent my last Christmas in Cold Spring. Then when the new year hit, so did catastrophe and I haven't been able to face it since, but this year, Dylan gave me the courage.

I stepped into the living room. It was the one part of the house untouched. Wood paneling still stretched across the walls leaving only room in the middle of one wall for the stone fireplace. To the left of the roaring fire were a bare Christmas tree and an oversized chair lined in red velvet. That was Santa's chair. It was a popular picture spot for most of the holiday season. Guests of the B&B would take their turns in the chair and even townsfolk would dress up and come in to use the chair and the fire as the perfect backdrop for their Christmas cards. The real magic of the red velvet chair in the living room though came to life on Christmas Eve. That's when Santa came for the annual "Cookies with Santa" event my mom and dad started more than a decade ago. My mom would line up her famous sugar cookies and pitchers of milk on a table along the wall. Everyone in Cold Spring would pack themselves in. Children would wait impatiently to tell Santa what they hoped he'd bring them the next morning and then they'd decorate a sugar cookie or two to place next to a bowl full of carrots in their own homes before they went to sleep. I was staring at the red chair with a huge smile on my face when I heard a creek on the floorboard behind me. I turned around to see Victoria and Dylan in the doorway.

"Can I hold him?" I asked, reaching out to Victoria.

"Sure! You can change him too if you want. My old room has all his stuff in it."

I pulled Dylan from her grasp and walked down the long hallway that led to the back of the house. The downstairs had three rooms, which was perfect for our family of four. Victoria's old room was the first one you came to after you passed the welcome desk. I pushed open the door on the left-hand side of the hallway. It was still painted the same mint green. Her queen-size bed that was once covered in a floral print comforter was now a simple off white. A bassinet was beside it. I laid Dylan down on the changing table next to the closet and fumbled through the baskets underneath to find a diaper.

Victoria moved out of this room five years ago when she married Trent. They now had a house of their own near the farmer's market a little outside of town. She helped a lot at the bed and breakfast these days, so she needed a place for Dylan to take his long afternoon nap.

"Hi, little guy." I tickled his now bare stomach as he squirmed underneath my grasp. His toothless smile grew bigger as I tucked his diaper under him. "Aren't you just the cutest thing I've ever seen?" He let out a little laugh as I struggle to button his footed tiger pajamas. "Are you going to be a soccer player?" I finally got the last button to snap in between his heavy kicks.

"Don't say that out loud when Trent is around." I turned to see Victoria walking through the door. "He wants him to play baseball, but the way he was kicking nonstop while still in here," she rubbed her palm against her stomach, "soccer seems the more appropriate path."

"My lips are sealed, but I can understand why daddy would want his son to follow in his footsteps."

Trent had been a ballplayer since little league. He now plays for a semi-pro team right here in the Hudson Valley. That means for half of the year he's on the road more than he's home, which has been a blessing for my mother these past few years when she's needed a helping hand. Victoria would never admit it, but she liked the company while Trent was gone.

"It's really good to have you home Addie. I know it hasn't been easy on you, these past few years."

Dylan sat on my hip with his tiny fingers entangled in my hair. I could feel the emotion welling up in my eyes as Victoria stepped closer. She reached in and enfolded the both of us in her grasp. We stood like that for some time before she finally broke the silence.

"If you need to talk, you know where to find me," she said.

I appreciated that. I had always been one to run from my feelings. Like a turtle, I hid behind my shell of armor. When I was feeling threatened, hurt, or alone, I would retract from the world and those around me. That's how I'd spent the last few years but coming home I'd realized how much I needed to talk. Before I could open up to Victoria or my mother though, there was someone else I needed to talk to first.

4

Addie

I reveled in the softness of my bedsheets my first night back home. The sweet smell of lavender on my pillowcase made it easy to drift off to sleep. Hudson found his spot curled up on the pillow next to me.

The house was still quiet when I woke up the next morning, but I was wide awake. I stretched my arms to meet the warmth of the window, a faux comfort that the sun outside was warming up the New York winter.

I knew that my mom would be in the kitchen making breakfast for the couple that occupied one of the bedrooms upstairs. It was the only room we had booked, but by the weekend, folks from the city would fill each one. Before I jumped in to help with front desk duties and cleaning, there was somewhere I wanted to go. I ran Hudson out the back quickly before pulling out a pair of light jeans and tucking a wool sweater into the waistband. It was the first of many layers I'd use to keep me warm. When I was ready to head out, Hudson was lying on my bed with a chew toy. I patted him on the head and closed the door behind me before slipping past Sue to the front door.

The sun had melted some of the snow off the sidewalks. There was now a stream running underneath my boots, but most of what fell last night was still settled on the grass. There must have been at least six inches on each side of me as I splashed my way to the village.

My favorite coffeehouse was on the corner of Main and Garden Street. Mave's Coffeehouse was the only place for coffee on the block when I was growing up. Two others had popped up in town over the last five years, but Mave's was still my favorite. I don't tell anyone that for comraderies' sake, but I think Mave knows.

When I stepped inside, it was as if I was eighteen again. The bright yellow walls surrounded me with the pink and white floral mural still painted on the wall above a line of wooden booths. The same white tables and chairs decorated the room where I had spent most of my high school days studying. I took in the fresh scent of blueberries baked into the muffins that hid underneath the glass tops of cake stands on the front counter. Back in the day, those blueberry muffins were one of maybe three items on the menu, but as my eyes scrolled up over the bakery selection, I could see clearly that the bed and breakfast wasn't the only thing that had changed in three years. There was now a wall-length chalkboard hung behind the counter. An expansive list of breakfast choices and wraps filled every inch of it in colorful cursive.

"Addie?" I heard a voice call. "Addie, is that you?"

I followed the sound of the voice to see Mave appear through a doorway that must have been constructed sometime within my absence. Her reddish hair was pulled back into a bun. A net held the loose pieces underneath.

"It's me, Mave!" I smiled. She slapped her hands over her mouth and her eyes shot wide as she quickly walked around from the back of the counter.

"Oh, Addie." Mave's eyebrows raised. She reached over and squeezed my shoulders. I watched her brown eyes burrow into me, observing everything that has changed. My dark brown hair was lighter. My bangs have grown out, and the strands that once fell below my shoulders now tangled at my chin. "We've missed you around here. How are you?" Mave asked.

"I'm doing alright. Living the big city life, you know," I said. I extend a kind smile in her direction.

"I have heard all about it. Your mother keeps us all in the loop."

Mave's hands slid behind my shoulders and she pulled me in for a hug. Her hand rested against the back of my head the same way my mothers always did. I could feel the wetness creep into my eyes. The realization of my time away hit me while my head leaned against the tip of Mave's chin. Before I let any of my tears slip down my cheek, I wiggled from her grasp and changed the subject.

"It looks like you're doing well too. Look at this place." I lifted my hands over my head and spun around to see it all. "You sure have been busy."

"Yes well, I can't take all the credit for it. With all the traffic coming in from the city these days, I knew it was time for a change. I wasn't sure what kind of a change until Drake came along."

One thing about growing up in a place like Cold Spring is that while you're here, you're desperately trying to find a way out. Then, once you leave, you find yourself gravitating back. Unless, of course, you're like me and the memories hurt too much to relive, but being back here now I could feel it. This place was home. The people, they weren't only shop owners and neighbors, they were family, and when your family consists of two thousand people you see every week, you come to know them all too well. That's why I shook my head at Mave. Drake was not part of this family, not the one I had grown up with. His name didn't sound the least bit familiar, and yet he'd transformed a staple in this town that may hold more memories for me than my own home.

5

Drake

I heard Mave's voice trail in through the kitchen. She must be talking to herself again. She always did that when she was updating the specials on the chalkboard. I was too distracted to fully understand her words as I placed the final pieces of fruit atop the masterpieces in front of me. I was getting good at this. Presentation was everything when it came to baking. Funny how it ranked even higher than taste, but I had no doubt that these babies were going to be delicious. These lemon tarts were part of a secret menu I'd been working on for weeks. I slipped the spoon between my lips and savored the perfect ratio of lemon juice, sugar, and my one secret ingredient — wait, I can't tell you that!

The lemon filling was now sitting inside the shortbread crust, and the specks of lemon zest and fresh blueberries topped it all off nicely. All I needed now was a taste tester, a role that Mave never objected to. I wiped the excess flour from my hands and sprinted to the front of the quiet coffeehouse.

"Hey Mave, you've gotta try...oh, I'm sorry. I didn't realize anyone was out here with you." I leaned back against the wall behind the counter. My eyes fixated on the shy smile of the girl standing next to Mave. The waves of her brown hair were peeking out from underneath a white knitted headband. The way the sun hit through the window exposed hits of caramel throughout her curls. Her gloves matched her headband as did the scarf that hung around her neck. I wandered my glance away from her smile long enough to notice the knee-high boots that covered her jeans. They were snug against her small frame but showed off her long, lean legs well.

When my concentration finally broke, I looked back up to find her honey-colored eyes staring into me. I swore if I drew a straight line it would connect with my bicep contracting underneath my white chef coat as I rubbed the sweat from my brow. I'd only been in Cold Spring for about a year, but I'd met everyone in this town twice over within the first few months. *Her* though... I had never seen her before.

"Addie, this is Drake." Mave thinned the air of mystery that stood between the two of us. "I hired him last year to help expand this little coffeehouse into a full-blown café."

Mave said her name as if it were familiar to her. I pulled the white hat from my head and tucked it under my arm as I crept out from behind the counter. Addie's shy smile grew. Her hand swept the waves of hair from her eyes. When I was close enough, I reached out my hand.

"It's nice to meet you," I said. Her hand was soft, but cold when I took it in mine.

"Likewise," she said. I could see the judgment by the way she tilted her head at me. I was the stranger in my own café.

"Addie is visiting from the city. She grew up here. I remember all the days she spent right over there, her headphones in and her eyes burrowed in a stack of books."

Mave was talking about the table in the far corner of the café. It sat tight against the wall, surrounded by windows on both sides. There was no better spot if you enjoyed people watching, which was something I had become fond of since moving to Cold Spring. There is nothing like city-goers visiting a quaint upstate town. They walk by with their narrow eyes pressed almost as tightly as the lips around their cigarettes. Don't get me wrong, I hold no issue with the travelers who keep this town's heart beating, but there is quite a difference between a New Yorker from the concrete jungle and a New Yorker from the rural pastures of upstate. From what I could tell in her glossed over smile and firm handshake, Addie still seemed to exude the roots of her small-town heritage.

"I hear you're the man behind the magic here," she smiled.

I liked the sound of that even if I couldn't take all the credit. It was a leap of faith for Mave. The same day I came across the ad, I came strolling into the coffeehouse in a pair of brown boots, worn-out jeans, and a blue cotton shirt. The sleeves hid the arm tattoo stained to my right forearm. Mave didn't even blink an eye when I told her why I had come. She reached in and grabbed one of the salted caramel brownies from the tin that sat in the front seat of my pickup for the forty-minute drive from New Paltz and took a bite. I was hired before she even finished that brownie, and to this day, she's never asked me to put on pair of shinier shoes or hike up the collar on my shirt so the ink on my shoulder blades doesn't show. Mave never made me feel as if I needed to apologize for who I was. She let me do what I did best, and according to Addie, that was magic. It seemed like the appropriate time to show both of them how magical it was.

"Well, you came at the right time Ms. Addie," I said. "I just finished a test run of lemon tarts and need some opinions. Hang tight."

I sprinted back behind the counter and grabbed the tray of tarts from the metal table in the kitchen. My walk back out was much slower. There was no way I was jeopardizing these yellow bits of perfection.

"These are all made in house." I heard Mave say as my steps grew closer to the door. "Drake has been a godsend to this place. His baking has pretty much doubled our business over the last eight months."

"That's amazing!" The rise in Addie's voice had me believe she meant it. For some odd reason, her approval made me smile. Maybe it's because to her, I'm the new kid in a tightknit family, and I desperately wanted to belong.

"Not to mention, he's good eye candy for the customers. Don't you think?"

Did those words come out of Mave's mouth? My brown boot took one more step before I glued it to the ground. I leaned my head a little closer to the open door. They couldn't see me where I stood, but I was intrigued to see what Addie's answer would be. I should've known that I wasn't going to get that kind of satisfaction.

"Mave!" Addie screeched in a loud whisper. Laughter followed, and I felt that was a good time for me to reappear.

"Alright ladies, try one of these."

Their laughter vanished when their eyes saw a dollop of freshly made whipped cream under a sprinkle of lemon zest.   Mave reached over first. Addie followed. I watched both of their eyes roll back once they bit into the shortbread crust.

"Wow!" Mave said. She swiped her tongue across her bottom lip then took the last bite of creamy lemon custard.

"This is delicious," Addie said. I reached the tray out closer to her. She snatched another one without hesitation. "If I still lived here, I'd have gained fifteen pounds by now. These are addicting."

I let out a huff that quickly turned into a chuckle. I knew that feeling all so well. That's why I give myself an extra hour in the morning. Six days a week

I'd run along the Hudson in anticipation of all the calories I knew I'd consume with recipe testing.

"I definitely eat my body weight in this stuff," I said. Her eyes wandered down my chef coat and back up again. "If I didn't work out, I'd be wearing it right here." I proudly patted the firmness of my abs. I worked hard for those lines. Addie snapped her head away from me, but not soon enough that I didn't notice the flush of color appear on her cheeks. I motioned again for her to take another one, but she waved her hands at me.

"No way. Two is my limit," she said. "I have to get going anyway. I've got somewhere I need to stop before my day begins."

"Mocha latte to go?" Mave asked.

"You know it."

I set the now half-empty tray on the table in front of me while Mave headed back to whip up the order from behind the counter. Addie swayed next to me. Her eyes stared at the ground. The flush of pink was still on her cheeks. I pulled at my earlobe, trying to think of something to say, but right as the courage inside me began to stir, Mave slipped the cup through a coffee sleeve and handed it over to Addie. *Darn you Mave,* I thought to myself as I shuffled the toe of my boot across the floor.

"This one is on me," Mave said.

"Oh no, Mave. I couldn't."

"Nonsense. Your loyalty earns you a free coffee now and then."

Addie's smile grew. Mave reached around her and pulled her in for a hug. Before she let go, she leaned down and whispered into Addie's ear, "tell him I said hi."

"I will." She smiled. I rubbed my chin sheepishly wondering who *he* was in that sentence. I made a mental note to ask Mave later as I backpedaled to the counter. Addie turned toward me. Her hand waving at me was once again covered with her white mitten.

"It was nice to meet you, Drake."

I saw her getting closer to the column in the middle of the room. I opened my mouth to throw out a warning. "Addie, watch the..." it was too late. Her chest had already felt the impact, and I watched as she bounced like a tennis ball off a racket. I slapped my hand over my mouth mostly to hide the smirk across my face. "Are you okay?" I asked, but I'm pretty sure her pride was hurt more than any part of her body

"That wasn't embarrassing at all," she said.

"I didn't see a thing." I winked. She knew I did. Thankfully, Mave and I were able to hold in the laughter until Addie was safely back outside into the brisk air.

6

Addie

I slapped my hand to my forehead once I was no longer in view of Mave's. "Way to go, Addie," I grunted.

I'd always had a way of making a memorable first impression on good looking boys. In high school, I sat two rows away from the quarterback of the football team. He had transferred midyear from Westchester. Two weeks in and I'd only had the pleasure of eyeing the back of his head. That was until the bell rang and I stood up. My feet were moving forward, but my eyes were deep down into my backpack. I can't even remember what I was searching for, but it had distracted me enough that when he stopped outside the classroom door, I didn't notice. I kept walking and shoved myself right into him. The back of his head I'd grown to know so well disappeared and his deep blue eyes were staring narrowly in my direction. I apologized profusely, but all he did was laugh. We dated for a few months after that. Not that I wanted to date Drake. I knew nothing about him, but being that he was the first good looking guy to walk into this tiny town that I didn't graduate with or play hide-and-seek down by the riverfront with when I was five, I would've hoped to have left a better impression.

The village streets were quiet this morning. It was a Thursday, so it wasn't a surprise. By midday tomorrow they'd be full of tourists. I loved and hated the attraction to Cold Spring. Tourism kept this town alive. Its rich history, pristine hiking views, and quaint shops would fascinate me too if I desired an escape from the city. They still fascinated me after all these years, but as I walked further down Main Street I took in the serenity. I had missed the peace and quiet of a frigid winter day. I was lucky that the world's escape was my hometown and was somewhat angry with myself at the way I'd neglected it these past few years. How dare I turn my back on a town that had been nothing but good to me. I knew no one judged me, but at that moment, I was judging myself.

I brushed off the snow that had collected on the arm of my jacket and stepped into Millie's Flower Shop that was located right at the end of the town's main strip. I asked for a mix of calla lilies and daisies. Millie made up a small bouquet for me. She didn't ask any questions, and she too refused to take any monetary compensation for my order. She simply wrapped a yellow bow around the stems and placed it in my free hand. The wetness that filled my eyes was all the thanks I could muster, but she understood. She nodded. I hugged the flowers tightly as I walked back out the door.

A few more blocks and I was walking through the black gate into a large open field. I could see the pops of color scattered around the fallen snow as I walked down the one paved trail that ran through. My scarf covered most of my face as the wind blew heavy past me. The tip of my nose was peeking out above the soft cotton and was taking the brunt of the glacial temperatures that December brought to upstate New York. I sipped my latte sparingly, trying to hang on to the warmth as long as I could. The cold had seeped through the thin layer of my jeans by the time I found the familiar stone. I tried to ignore it as I bent down.

"Hi, Daddy." I brushed the snow off the stone to reveal the words: *beloved husband and father.* I remember all the nights my mother sat scribbling on a notepad in the front living area of the B&B. She was trying to figure out the right words to place on his headstone, but no matter what she wrote it never seemed enough. I stared at the wording we chose. It still didn't seem like enough, but it was the truth. It was simple, and my dad wouldn't have wanted us to make a big fuss anyway. He hated having the attention on him. He spent his whole life doing for others. Like when I was too afraid to leave home to attend my dream college in Boston. When I first received my acceptance letter, I tucked it into the top drawer of my nightstand. I pretended I didn't get my acceptance letter to Boston and that I would just stay close to home. *I'll go to Vassar.* That's what I told him. Vassar was an amazing college and I would be so lucky to get my education from there.

"Vassar is a great school, but it's not your dream school," he said to me. My father had a way of making everything seem less scary. The monsters under my bed, my first heartbreak, and then my going away to college. Even with a B&B to run, he still made it up to Boston every other weekend until I was no longer afraid to be on my own. It seemed ironic that a man with the biggest heart I'd ever known, was no longer here because that same heart gave up on him.

"I'm sorry it's taken me so long." I reached down and placed the bouquet underneath his name. The tears that had escaped my eyes were now icicles on my cheeks. "It's so hard to be here without you."

It was a cold day like today when I received the call from my mother. I had only been living in the city for a few months at that point. My first Christmas since graduation had come and gone and we were in the depths of winter. My job, the same one I had now, was running me ragged. I loved it back then. It was my first big girl job. The steppingstone to a successful career in the fashion world. That's what I thought anyway. All of it came to a halt that mid-February morning. Through her sobs, she muttered the words.

Your father, he's gone.

I think that was the worst part of all of this. I didn't get to say goodbye. One minute he was here and the next he was gone. I had come up for the funeral, but the sheer weight of sadness and anger that fell upon me that day had kept me hidden away in the city until now. I put all of my energy into work and until I stepped off that train yesterday afternoon, I didn't realize what all that sadness had me missing.

"I bet you know about Dylan." My hand continued to clear the snow. "He's the cutest thing. Trent wants him to be a baseball player. Can you believe mom finally painted those railings white like you always wanted? You were right. It made a world of difference. I'm sure mom knows, but she'll never admit it."

I laughed and I swear in the whisper of the wind that brushed across my ears, I could hear his as well. It was so vivid that it made my tears flow harder. The sun was peeking through the bareness of the tree branches. I could feel its warmth, but it wasn't enough to stop my cheeks from succumbing to the frigid breeze.

"I'm going to be around more often. I promise." I placed my damp glove against my lips and then pressed it against the stone where his name was carved. *Gregory John Pine.* "I love you, Daddy."

I pushed myself back up and gave my legs a minute to release the tension of holding my body weight. I brushed the wetness from my face and let out a heavy sigh before I stepped back onto the path. The open-air felt like freedom against my skin as I walked back to the B&B. There were no buildings to block the sunlight or loud horns bouncing off the maze of cars that usually met me on my morning commute. It was just me, the smell of fresh snow, a cold breeze, and a new outlook that I didn't know I'd been longing for.

7

Addie

I sat at the kitchen table later that evening stuffing gingerbread into boxes and tying them closed with bits of red and green ribbon. They were the welcome gifts for tomorrow's guests. Every month mom always had something new to give. Last time I'd been home she was giving little cones of hot cocoa mix.

"These cookies look amazing. Did you bake them?" I asked.

"Not these. I got them from Mave's. She has all sorts of things there now." Mom yelled from the other side of the wall. She was in the kitchen preparing the menu for tomorrow's dinner.

"Yes, I saw that when I went over there this morning."

I saw mom peek around from the other side of the wall. She had a smirk plastered across her face. "Did you meet Drake?" she asked. I watched her saunter over to me with raised eyebrows.

"Yes, I met Drake." I slid the plate of cookies closer to her as she sunk in the chair next to me. She grabbed a box from the middle of the table and we simultaneously stacked the cookies one by one.

"And…isn't he cute?"

"Mother! I narrowed my eyes in her direction.

"What? I'm just saying."

"Next thing you're going to *just say* is that he's single too isn't it?" I shook my head. It was obvious what she was doing. This was like that time in high school when Corey Barnham moved across the river from New Paltz. Mom met him and his mother at the grocery store about a week after he started at school. She came home with that same smirk on her face. *Have you met the new kid?* She asked me. *He'll probably need a date to the prom.* Funny enough I did end up going to the prom with Corey, but only as friends and not at all because of my mother's nagging.

"I wasn't going to say that," she said, "but since you mentioned it, Mave said he does live alone."

"Oh, my gosh mother!" I whipped one of the pieces of red ribbon over at her. The air caught it and it ended up drifting to the floor between us. "I've been home all of two minutes and you're already trying to set me up."

I looked over to see the corners of her eyes droop and the smirk that once lined her lips disappear. She reached over for another cookie and her shoulders sunk as she slid it into the box. My chest tightened.

"I'm sorry mom," I said. "I didn't mean that. I know your intentions are good. It's just…I have a lot going on right now with a new dog, my job and still healing from dad."

She put her arm around me. I felt the pressure on my arm as she pulled me toward her. Her lips pressed against my forehead. "I know honey." She kissed me one more time before letting go.

By that time all the cookie boxes were filled. I flipped the top of the last one closed and stacked them all on top of each other. All I had to do now was get the room keys and set them inside each room with a handwritten note from my mom. I squeezed the boxes in between my hands as I walked to the backroom to grab the keys. The distance must have made her brave because right as I pulled the first key down from the wall I heard her voice from the other room.

"He is pretty cute though, isn't he?"

I gave in. She deserved for me to humor her. I gripped the keys in one hand while still firmly holding the boxes of cookies in the other. "Yes mother, he is *very* cute."

The smile was back on her face. I ran upstairs and set the cookies in all four of the rooms. The couple from Long Island had checked out early that morning and the cleaning service had come and gone. All rooms were now ready for tomorrow's visitors who most likely were heading up for the town's pop up Christmas festival that would take over the village square. I locked the door behind me and headed back downstairs where mom was tapping away at the keyboard behind the front desk.

"Are you going to be able to make the Christmas festival?" I asked her. I knew she was doing a lot on her own these days. She had given Sue the next couple of days off to finish up her shopping. "I can hang here tomorrow if you need me to."

"Nonsense." She waved her hand at me. "You should go have fun. Your sister wants to bring Dylan. You can go with her."

"Where is Trent?" I asked.

"He'll be back in town on Sunday. Went up to visit his dad in Albany. You know, the child of divorced parents. They trade on and off who comes to visit here each year. This year his mom is coming to town.

"Ah, gotcha. Are you sure you don't want to go?" I asked. She nodded.

"I'm sure. I may even be able to sneak out for a few after dinner." I think she could tell by the way my eyes beamed that I was thankful.

Gosh, I missed that festival. Don't get me wrong. New York City is magical at Christmas time. I am still mesmerized by the holiday window displays, the tree lighting at Rockefeller Center, and ice skating in Bryant Park. The holiday markets also dazzle, but Christmas in Cold Spring had been enchanting for as far back as I can remember. Santa Claus always made surprise visits on his sleigh throughout December. He'd come with a sack full of candy canes and hand them out to every child after they whispered their Christmas wishes in his ear.

The stars weren't the only thing that lit up the sky at night. There were strands of lights hung all over town. The gazebo down by the river was always one of my parent's favorite places for Christmas card photos. Every year we may have grown older, and our clothes would be different, but the background never changed.

Being gone for the last couple of years, I was excited to see if the Christmas festival still brought the same enchantment over me.

The final Friday before Christmas, shops along Main Street stayed open late. Some set up tables outside with drinks, snacks, and fun trinkets from their stores. There were arts and crafts for both adults and children. Carolers walked the streets with their sheet music in hand. I was beyond excited to throw myself back into that winter wonderland.

"How about you and I grab some dinner before all the craziness starts?" Mom asked. I knew there wasn't going to be much time for it to be just mom and me. Victoria was over a lot now and once Trent's mom got into town everyone would be over here canoodling the baby.

"I'd like that," I said.

"How about pizza?"

My eyes widened. "Yes! Gus's or Salvatore's?" I asked. If you wanted to witness one of the biggest family debates in my family's history, it would be over pizza. It was always a family divided. Dad and I loved Gus's and Mom and Victoria were all about Salvatore's. It took at least a half-hour on those nights to make a decision. The choice always came down to rock, paper, scissors.

Mom held out her hand to me. That same smirk she gave when asking about Drake was back. "Are you ready?" she asked. I lifted my hand so it was even with hers.

"Ready!"

It was the best of three and I'm pretty sure mom let me win. We followed my screech of victory to the door. We wrapped ourselves up in our winter coats and I tugged my hat over my head before I headed out the door. Mom slipped her arm through mine, and the two of us walked boisterously into the brisk wind to enjoy the best pizza in town.

8

Drake

I missed the Friday festival last year. Mave let me have the week of Christmas off so I could go back to New Paltz and spend the holidays with my family. When I returned, it was two weeks straight of customers saying, "I can't believe you missed it," that made me determined to be here this year.

It took some convincing. My parents weren't the happiest when I announced my acceptance into culinary school. The frowns on their faces grew even more apparent when I dropped the, *I'm moving to Cold Spring to work at a coffeehouse,* bomb. I was their son though and I might not have been the favorite between my brother and me right now, but when I put my foot down this year, they folded. My parents would be arriving in Cold Spring on the 23rd. So, tonight, I planned to experience the Friday festival like a real townie.

Mave and I closed up shop to the coffeehouse around 6:30p.m. The sky had been dark for hours now, but the red bow wrapped streetlamps that lined Main Street were so bright it was as if the sun had yet to set on the small town I now called home. I smoothed out the black cloth draped over the table in front of the shop.

"I hope you're ready for tonight," Mave said.

"Oh, I'm ready. How does it feel having someone else join in on your fifteen-year tradition?" I asked.

"Technically, it's a twenty-five-year tradition if you count the years my pops was here pouring each cup by hand."

I had heard the story more than a dozen times since I'd started working with Mave. Since she was eight years old, she would stand in her red apron and matching hair bow behind this very same table. Like a hawk, she'd eye the toppings and make sure they were always full for people to scoop into their cups of hot cocoa. When they'd run low, she'd dive under the table for the refills and replenish the low stock. I adored Mave's love for her coffeehouse. I loved the little traditions she kept alive for her father and the bravery it took for someone like me to come in and make changes. I respected the history of the coffeehouse, and in implementing what I felt would help keep the business alive, I was still careful to preserve what made it special.

Mave plopped down two large crockpots. I was still new to Mave's inner circle which meant she wasn't going to tell me what made up her stellar concoction. I was able to convince her to let me have a crockpot of my own. She hesitated at first. When I asked, she scoffed with her arms folded, but after a bite of one of my dark chocolate peanut butter cookies, she gave in. All the ingredients for my cocoa were tucked in a plastic bin underneath the table. In thirty minutes, I'd start piecing it all together.

"Do you think we'll need more cups?" I asked. Mave eyed the two rows of red and Green cups stacked in front of me.

"Most likely, but I have a couple of boxes in the storage closet. When we get close, I'll run and grab them."

"So, this festival..." I said, "everyone in town comes to it?"

"Everyone who's anyone." Mave's hands gripped the plastic on the bag of marshmallows and yanked it open. It was only one of the many toppings we would have lined up. "If you're referring to a certain everyone though, I can't make any promises."

I brushed my hands across the sides of my dark jeans hoping to wipe away any bead of sweat that had formed. I wasn't trying to be obvious, but Mave read right through me. Still, I was going to play it off. Desperation didn't look good on me.

"I wasn't referring to anyone in particular," I said. "I was curious, that's all."

"Mhmm, and does your curiosity happen to involve a young brunette named Addie."

My eyes flew wide at the sound of her name and I tried desperately to blink back any motion of pleasure that it gave me. I'd only spent five minutes with her, and for most of it, I watched her salivate over my lemon tarts. Those five minutes were all it took for me to want more.

I liked that she had an interest in my tarts. I also couldn't help but notice her genuine love for Mave's and the fact that she took notice of all my creative add-ons.

"It didn't, but since you brought her up, what's her story?" I asked.

I pretended to focus my attention on counting out a stack of napkins, but the straight line of Mave's lips turned upward once those words came out of my mouth.

"What do you mean?" she asked.

"I dunno. You've just never mentioned her before, and I'm surprised I haven't seen her around for as long as I've been here."

"I told you, she lives in the city."

"Well yea, but has she not come back to visit at all?"

Mave's cheeks suddenly grew pale. She pressed her lips together tightly and hurriedly shook out the ends of the already smoothed out linen. I felt a lump in my throat. What an idiot I was for trying to push the subject. I could tell by Mave's stern response to Addie living in the city that I was entering uncharted territory.

"It's not my place," Mave said. I nodded and quickly changed the subject to hot cocoa, but the twinge of curiosity hung in my mind. What kind of secret could the girl with innocent eyes and a shy smile be hiding?

9

Addie

Dylan didn't seem to be phased by the noise around him as he slept in his stroller in the middle of Friday's pop-up festival. Victoria and I started our Friday evening sitting under a white tent in the middle of Main Street. She was cutting out tiny pink hearts from construction paper and I was rifling through a pile of Christmas themed stickers.

"I always loved this Christmas card making booth," I said. I pulled a Christmas tree sticker from its backing and placed it on the front of my nicely folded red construction paper.

"I feel the same. It's been lonely the last couple of years without you." Victoria didn't look over at me. She swiped the glue on the back of her pink hearts and placed them inside of her card.

"I know," I said. "I'm sorry, but I'm here now." I glanced over to see a smile growing from behind the strands of chestnut hair falling in front of her face.

"You are the best present I could've asked for. I know that Mom thinks the same," she said.

My eyes widened and I felt my lips curl up as I reached for the scissors that lay on the table between us. The fluttering in my stomach was proof of how happy I was to be home. I didn't expect it to be as easy as it was. I looked around at the crowds of people gathering in the middle of the village. The carolers were singing in front of the hardware store and the line for Santa stretched for two blocks. It was all still familiar to me. It was as if I'd never left.

The card-making table was full of laughter. Next to me were two young girls. They couldn't have been more than seven. Their mother was helping them spell out Merry Christmas as they wrote the letters in green marker. I didn't recognize her, but with it being the weekend, the local to visitor ratio was highly uneven by this point.

I wrote the final words down inside my card.

Love always, Addie.

I placed the marker down in front of me and pressed along the seal of the card one last time. In an effort to be discreet, I slowly leaned down closer to the bag that was on the floor beside me. My fingers grasped the zipper and pulled it to the other side. I grabbed the camera that sat inside and leaned back to get a good shot of my work of art. I turned over to see Victoria's nose scrunched as she stared intently at the pink heart on the front of her card. She rotated it in one direction and then the other, trying to decide the perfect place to glue it down.

Click. She heard me freeze her moment in time.

"Did you just take my picture?"

I peered around from the back of the camera and shrugged with a smile on my face. I looked over at Dylan. He was still sound asleep underneath the thick blue blanket my mom had knitted for him. Adjusting the camera lens for a clear view, I snapped a photo to document Dylan's first holiday pop-up.

I snapped a few more photos of the scene around me while I waited for Victoria to finish.

"Alright! I'm all done," Victoria said. She gathered her do-it-yourself cards into a neat pile and slid them into the side pocket of Dylan's diaper bag. "I think my fingers turned into icicles," she laughed. "I can barely move them."

"Mine too," I said. I walked over the heater just outside the tent and rubbed my hands back and forth until my palms absorbed the heat. Victoria did the same. Once both of us had feeling back in our fingers, I tightened the scarf around my neck and slipped my gloves back on.

"How about we hit up the hot cocoa bar?" Victoria asked.

"I could use some hot cocoa," I said.

Mave's hot cocoa bar was famous in this neck of the woods. Anyone who came up for the Christmas festival knew they couldn't leave without a cup of Mave's hot cocoa in their hands. Victoria and I tried over the years to guess the secret ingredient that made her hot cocoa so special, but Mave would always squeeze her thumb and pointer together and zip them across her lips. Whatever it was, after years of being deprived, I was ready for a nice big cup topped with whipped cream, marshmallows, and all the toppings.

"So, tell me, how's the city been treating you these past few years?" We were standing behind a line of about a dozen people when those words flooded from Victoria's mouth.

"It's great," I said. "There's never a dull moment. We're getting ready to launch our spring collection and there's a photoshoot as soon as I get back." I had always been good at making my assistant job sound more glamorous than it was. "My friend Brody has been giving me photography lessons and I feel like I'm really coming into my own. It'll come in handy down the road for sure."

"Oh, Brody?" Victoria tried to nudge her elbow into my side but I had on too many layers. "Is he cute?" Her eyelashes fluttered with sarcasm.

I took a quick photo of the kids that were skipping by us. They held each other's hands as they leaped up into the air with every step. The distraction gave me enough time to think of how I would answer.

"He is super cute!" I said. "I don't think I'm quite his type though."

"What? Why? Who wouldn't like you?" Victoria's hands pushed Dylan's stroller back and forth as her voice squealed.

"Let's just say I think he prefers to date someone who doesn't have..." I tapped my hands across my chest to bring attention to the big difference between a man and a woman.

"Ohh! I see." Victoria's eyes widened. "Well, I'm glad you found a good friend in the city either way."

"I definitely have," I said.

The conversation ended there because it was finally our turn to fill our cups with hot cocoa. Mave was standing behind the black tablecloth, scooping a ladle from the crockpot. Standing next to her was Drake. He was emptying mini marshmallows into an empty glass jar. My eyes moved from the marshmallows to the thin layer of stubble that traced around his jawline. It matched perfectly with the stand of sandy brown hair that was peeking out from underneath his cotton hat.

"Hello, girls! It's so lovely to see you together again." Mave's voice pulled me from my gaze on Drake. She reached across the table with two cups and handed one to each of us. I grabbed on tight to mine and watched the steam from inside the cup rise quickly into the air. "And look at that little guy." She peered down into the stroller. "He's getting bigger by the minute."

"You don't have to tell me twice." Victoria swept her hand across the hat on Dylan's head. "I blinked and all of a sudden he doubled in size."

Mave laughed. "I know how that is." The line behind us was growing. "It was great to see you as always ladies. Now, go get your toppings." We waved goodbye to Mave and moved on down the table to where Drake was standing.

"Hey Drake!" Victoria said.

"Hey Victoria. How's the little guy doing?"

It would make sense that Victoria knew Drake. She too was a frequent customer of Mave's Coffehouse since her high school years.

"He's such a good baby," she said. "He's been sleeping through the night for almost a week now."

"I bet that is heavenly," Drake laughed. Victoria nodded. "Whipped cream?" He held a scoop over her cup.

"You know it," she said and let Drake pile it on. He looked over at me when he was done and asked the same thing. I nodded. "I'm so sorry! Have you met my sister yet?" Victoria asked. "This is Addie."

I could have spoken about our meeting the other day at the coffeehouse, but the words were lost on me as I watched my reflection in his eyes. Suddenly the frostiness that I had been feeling only moments ago had disappeared and I wasn't sure if it was the hot cocoa kicking in or the rapid beating of my heart that started once Drake's attention focused on me. The only thing I could move was my lips, so I perked them up into a half-smile.

"We have actually." I was thankful that Drake was able to speak for me. "I didn't realize you were Victoria's sister."

I slowly reached my hand out for a metal scoop that lay in front of the toppings. I shook it back and forth as tiny sprinkles of candy cane fell into my cup. I did the same for the chocolate chips, trying to calm my nerves. It was Victoria's turn to sprinkle toppings onto her hot cocoa. That left Drake and me to pick up the conversation.

"Yup! That's me." Alright, I know. It wasn't the most eloquent of words, but it was better than standing there with my mouth wide open staring at him. Which by the way, I continued to do after I responded.

"It's nice to see you again," Drake said. His smile showed off the whiteness of his perfectly lined teeth. I nodded once again because when Drake was around I seemed to have forgotten how to form words.

Pull yourself together Addie! I could hear my inner voice screaming. Victoria was still plopping marshmallows onto the top of her whipped cream. I looked over at Mave right as she jerked her glare away from us. She poured another ladle full of hot cocoa into a cup and called out to Drake.

"Why don't you take a break," she said. "You've been at this for a while."

"That's okay. I don't want to leave you to fend for yourself," he said.

"Oh honey, do you know how many years I've been pouring hot cocoa by myself?" Her hand was firm against her hip. "Go on now, have some fun."

"Alrighty then." Drake reached behind him to untie the apron around his waist. "Is it cool if I hang with you guys for a bit?"

It would figure that Victoria would mind her own business until she saw an opportunity. She set the metal scoop back down on the table and patted the top of Dylan's stroller. "I should probably be getting this guy to bed, but I'm sure Addie would love the company."

I didn't blink. My brown eyes burned into Victoria's as my breath grew heavier. She winked and almost as if she had planned it, Dylan's eyes shot open and his tiny mouth let out a cry.

"Yeah...yeah, of course," I stuttered. "I'd love the company."

"Great!" Drake lifted the bottom of the tablecloth and tossed his apron underneath. Mave waved at him and he took that as assurance that she'd be alright without him.

I leaned down, pulled the blanket down off Dylan's face enough to kiss the tip of his nose. Then leaned into Victoria's open arms.

"Have fun," she whispered. I could sense the hint of sarcasm in her voice. The one that solidified that she had some sort of plan for this.

"Don't get any ideas," I said back.

"Who me?" She let her arms fall to her side and I shook my head at the way her brows furrowed, trying to look innocent.

"Take good care of my sister Drake. I'll see you guys later." Victoria gave one last wave before she rolled Dylan's stroller away and left the two of us standing there by ourselves.

"Shall we," Drake motioned.

"Let's do it!" I could feel my nerves kicking in. That tingling sensation leaped from my chest to my stomach as the two of us wandered through the growing crowd. Maybe it was all the time I'd spent with Brody knowing I couldn't give in to his boyish good looks, but I couldn't stop staring at the scruff on Drake's jawline. I also loved the way his thick eyelashes lined across his deep-set eyes in a way that would make any girl jealous. Every time Drake lifted his cup to his lips, my eyes caught the contraction of his biceps underneath his gray sweater. He also received bonus points for choosing Cold Spring to settle down in and the fact that he worked for Mave, who was like a second mother to me. My eyes were still watching the movement underneath Drake's sweater when his voice echoed into my thoughts.

"So, how come I haven't seen you around town before?" Drake asked right as came up to the front of the General Store.

"Well..." I bought myself some time. I'm not sure I was ready to dive deep into the trenches of my father's heart attack with someone I barely knew. So, I settled for the familiar excuse I used to use when I disappointed my mother. "I live in the city and work has been kind of crazy. You're going a hundred miles an hour and before you know it, too much time has passed."

"I get that. I remember when I first started school at the CIA..." I didn't let him finish."

"You were in the CIA?!" My eyes widened. "Like Jack Ryan? I love that show!"

Drake's eyes crinkled as his voice grew bubbly. "Not that CIA. The Culinary Institute of America."

I slammed my palm against my forehead. "Duh, that totally makes sense." The Culinary Institute was a staple in the Hudson Valley. Settled in the historic town of Hyde Park, it was maybe a forty-five-minute drive from Cold Spring. "I promise I'm done interrupting your story with mindless banter," I laughed. "Go on."

"That's okay. I just get the timing thing. A year and a half at the CIA flew by. Before I knew it, I was pulling into Cold Spring having no idea what was waiting for me.

The two of us walked up the steps to the General Store. Drake pulled open the painted red door and I stepped onto the hardwood floor. The gust of warmth that met me at the entry thawed my frigid skin. I loosened the scarf around my neck as I walked over to a shelf lined with flavored jams. I reached for a jar of the vanilla bean pear.

"I make a killer thumbprint cookie with that jam," Drake said. "Oh, and this one," he reached over me to pull a jar of apple jalapeno down. "I stuffed this in a cinnamon donut over the fall. They sold like hotcakes."

"That sounds amazing. I'll take one." I snatched the jar from his hand with a wink.

"I see how it is," he laughed.

"So, what made you want to be a... baker?" My voice rose.

"Mave calls me the catering manager. It has a nice ring to it." He smiled and his lips parted once again to show his perfectly lined teeth. I nodded in agreement and turned toward the register to check out.

"Well, well, well...Miss Addie, I almost forgot what you looked like."

"Oh Frank, it hasn't been that long has it?" I set the two jars on the wood-grained counter. Frank was now the owner of The General Store. His father had put in every penny he owned to open the store back in the 1950s. When he passed away, Frank took over. Rumor has it he could've retired at least a decade ago, but loves the customers so much, he says he'll be cashing out for as long as the good Lord lets him.

"It's been too long, Addie. Way too long." Frank wrapped the jars and slid them into a paper bag with the store logo on the front. "Don't let it happen again, okay?" I nodded as my glove covered fingers grabbed the handles and swung the bag off the counter.

"Bye Frank!" I yelled as Drake met me with the open door.

Drake and I found an empty bench at the end of the street. I lowered myself down slowly and my body shook from the coldness that was seeping through my jeans. Drake settled in next to me. He rubbed his hands furiously together.

"Man, it is cold out tonight," he said. I nodded before taking a sip of my now lukewarm cocoa. "What do you do in the city?" Drake's body was turned toward me. His eyebrows lifted in anticipation of my answer, but it wasn't time for me yet. I was not letting him dodge the question I'd asked before we warmed up in the General Store.

"Wait a minute, you never told me what made you want to be a baker...I mean, catering manager? You go first."

He tugged at the black hat that covered his head. It was a total contrast from the color that hid underneath. I remember staring at it in the coffeehouse the day we met. Tiny curls were lined across his forehead.

"Honestly, it started out as a rebellion. My dad owns an auto shop back in New Paltz. I worked there all through high school with the expectation that it would be mine someday, but my hands wanted to do more than fix car parts. They wanted to create things."

Drake waved his hands wildly, but they didn't distract me from the sparkle in his eye when he talked about receiving the letter than would carve out a totally different path in his life. My face sunk when he got to the part where he told his parents.

"For three years after high school, I worked as a food runner at Mohonk. I needed a change of scenery and got to know the chefs really well. They let me work alongside them every now and then and I fell in love with how many ways you could cook a piece of chicken or season the bland out of vegetables."

Though I didn't spend much time in the dining room of Mohonk Mountain House, I was familiar with the popular destination when Drake brought it up. Breakneck Ridge here in Cold Spring was my favorite place to go hiking, but Mohonk was a close second. Dad and I went one weekend when I was in junior high and we got completely lost. Our one-hour hike up to the Gatehouse took about four hours and we never even made it there. My legs felt it for days. I couldn't help but smile as I thought about it.

"You traded oil rags for dish rags huh?" I smiled.

"Haha, I did. I applied to the CIA without telling my parents and when I got in my dad didn't talk to me for three weeks. He hated that I ruined his plan."

"Oh gosh, I'm so sorry. Is he still mad?" I asked.

I couldn't even imagine my dad not supporting me. When I wanted to be an Olympic swimmer, he and my mom traded off on the multiple drives a week up to Poughkeepsie for swim meets. I was a determined ten-year-old and I held the record for the 100m butterfly for years. A heaviness fell over me as I listened to Drake. Not because thinking of my dad made me sad, but because I wished he had the kind of support I always did from the man I looked up to.

"I wouldn't say mad. My younger brother stepped up to the plate, so he's less bitter, but every now and then he lets a snide remark slip about my life in the kitchen." I lifted my partially frozen fingertips to Drake's shoulder, and I could tell that he could see the sympathy in my eyes the way I looked longingly at him. "Enough about me though. It's your turn." He patted my leg with his hand. I winced at the way it stung from the bite of the winter air. "What is it that you do in the big old city?"

"I'm a web designer and budding photographer." I lifted my camera for him to see. "At least, that's what I moved to the city to be."

"And you're not doing that?" His face scrunched in confusion.

"I'm not getting paid for it anyway. It's more of a hobby. I'm a personal assistant right now, trying to climb my way up the ranks. I work in fashion, which I love. I do more of setting up the photoshoots and running errands to get the clothes than actually taking photos of the clothes and organizing them up on the website."

"It seems as if you're moving in the right direction. You're at least working in the industry. Right?"

Three years ago, I felt that way. I still remember my first day. I slung a bag full of desk décor over my shoulder. I walked through the front doors with a smile on my face and excitement surging through me. Now, I felt as if my life had become mundane. Others who sat in the office with me had moved on. Some moved upstairs to better jobs and others left for better opportunities.

"I've been in the same position for three years. There have been a lot of design jobs or photo editing jobs I've applied for, but without real experience, no one's willing to take a chance on me. How can I get experience if I can't get a job where I can learn?" I shrugged my shoulders. That was the one thing I hated about the job search. *We've decided to move forward with other candidates that more closely align with our needs.*

Every time I opened an email, that's what I read. How do you know I can't meet your needs? How am I supposed to even try if no one will give me a chance to prove myself? It was frustrating.

"Do you have a portfolio?" Drake asked.

"I'm starting to build one. I have a friend back in the city who's been helping me. Right now, it's filled with photos of Central Park and my dog. That's not quite what hiring managers want to see."

"What about food?" I tilted my head in Drake's direction. "I know it's not fashion, but culinary is such a huge market." Drake jumped up from the bench and clapped his hands together. "I have an idea! Why don't you come to Mave's on Sunday? We close at two, so maybe come then. We can set up a photoshoot. It'll help build your portfolio, and honestly, we could use the pictures. It'd be a win-win for both. What do you say?"

I had never really thought of working in the culinary field. Articles on restaurants and recipes were pretty big, but I'd always had my heart in fashion. I looked up at Drake's wide eyes and frozen smile. Even if I wanted to, those dimples on each cheek kept me from any objections. As I prepared my answer, I realized that Drake was right, broadening my horizons couldn't hurt any. Spending a little extra time looking into those hazel eyes was also a bonus.

"Yeah," I nodded. "Sunday at two. You have a deal." I jumped up and reached out my hand. Drake grabbed onto it. He must've felt me shivering because once he let go, he reached up and tugged at my scarf, so my skin wasn't exposed to the chilly temperatures of the sunless sky.

"That's better," he smiled. His hands brushed down the sides of my arms before they settled back against him. "I should probably get back to helping Mave. It looks like the line has really picked up over there."

He pointed through the crowd. I leaned past his broad stature to see that the line had doubled since Victoria and I had stood in it. Mave was bobbing from one side of the table to the other trying to keep up.

"Oh right. Yes, you should get back there. I should go let my dog out and see if my mom needs any help closing up for the night."

"I'll see you Sunday though," Drake said. He began to step backward toward the crowd.

"Yes, I will see you Sunday."

I waved at him before he turned himself away from me. Then I stood in that spot, frozen like the snow beneath me. That tingling had returned, but this time it wasn't nerves, it was excitement. I had a gig in two days. It wasn't a paying gig, and taking photos of cupcakes and baked goods weren't as glamorous as the fast-paced world of fashion photography, but it was something. It was a step in the right direction. Maybe it would help this design dream of mine come to life after all.

10

Addie

Sunday afternoon marked the end of the weekend for the New York City goers that spent the last couple of nights here in Cold Spring. I woke up early to help with breakfast. Living in a bed and breakfast for most of my life, I had grown accustomed to being a morning person. Breakfast started at 7:00 a.m. and usually, the roaring of voices escaped down the hallways into my bedroom not long after that.

The colleges in the area were now on winter break, so the part-time help my mother usually counted on had gone home until January. I took orders and delivered plates while my mom helped settle bills and take back the room keys. By eleven, the rooms were empty, and guests were lugging their suitcases down the stairs.

I yanked the sheets off the beds in all the rooms and replaced them with new ones. I folded under the bottom sheet the way my dad had taught me and slid my hands across to iron out the wrinkles. When the last room was finished, I stood admiring my work in the doorway with my hand squeezing the cold metal of the knob. The pillows were fluffed and ready for the arrival of the next set of guests. Ms. Simon, the owner of one of the antique shops in town, had her daughter coming for a couple of days. Her family was staying in one room and her in-laws in another. They'd be arriving in the morning which meant the B&B had a night of peace. It was rare this time of year to have openings, but it felt good to have the house to myself for at least one night. I heard the click of the door as I closed it behind me and briskly walked down the carpeted stairs to the blue velvet couch that sat in the entryway. It caught me as I fell onto it hard.

"I forgot how exhausting Sundays were," I sighed. My hands were too tired to move the hair that had fallen across my face. I blew a puff of hot air from between my lips and felt it sweep back over my ear. I hear my mother laugh.

"Don't I know it," she said. Her voice was faint. A gray-colored wall separated us. She was still in the dining area wiping down the last table. "Your father was always the bright and bubbly one in the mornings. I tended to hide behind the financials and reservation book until the coffee kicked in."

"Yes! He used to go around from table to table humming that...oh what was that song?!"

It was ingrained in my head now after all those years. I closed my eyes and my head fell into my hands as I hummed the melody, trying to remember the words. I should've known that my mother wouldn't have forgotten. Every little detail about my father was written in the journal she carried in her mind. She started belting out the lyrics. I could not believe I had forgotten.

Mr. Rogers was a staple in this house since before I could walk. My dad and I used to sit on the couch in the back living room when my childhood internal alarm clock had me up before the sun. He'd record the latest episode and I would curl up on his lap while it played.

I watched my mom from my spot on the blue couch as she danced around the living room. Her voice was so cheerful. The smile on her face was shining as bright as the lights that lined our cozy street at night. I jumped up and started dancing with her. My singing voice sounded more like the ghastly hoot of a barn owl that shudders you from a peaceful sleep, but neither of us cared.

My dad always had a way of bringing people together. As my mom and I trotted around the living room singing and laughing, I couldn't help but think that the warmth from the sunlight shining in through the window was somehow his way of saying, *I'm still here. I'm dancing with you.*

"Haha! Oh, I needed that," Mom said. She reached her arms out and I fell into them. I could feel her chest pushing against me forcefully with each breath she took. "My girl, I'm so glad you're home." She wheezed through each word and then pressed her lips on the top of my head.

"Me too," I said. She loosened her grasp. I looked up at her mane of brown curls.

"At least now you get to rest for the day. You should head down and take a walk by the river," she said.

"Maybe I will. Later though." I twisted my wrist to see the time on my watch. In a half-hour, Drake would be expecting me at the coffeehouse. "I have to head over to Mave's first."

"Mave's?" she asked. "What for?"

"Drake and I are going to do a little photoshoot for the shop. He thought it would be a good way to add to my portfolio."

The ruse of curiosity sparked in her eyes as her cheekbones raised. She tapped her pointer finger to my nose. Then came a sound from between her lips that resembled that of a hungry pig. I cringed, slamming my hands over my ears.

"It's a work thing. Don't get too excited."

"I didn't say anything." She didn't have to. Her reaction was enough to have me shaking my head.

I wasn't a cynic of love. Don't get me wrong. My parents were college sweethearts. They fell in love after an overthrown pass in my dad's quarterback days landed right on the side of my mother's face. Her pom-poms flew from her grasp as she clutched her face and fell to the grass. My father could never keep his composure when he told that story. His lively laugh pierced through the ears of anyone who was listening as my mother frowned, her eyes would narrow and she would cross her arms while she quietly waited for him to finish the story.

Real funny, she would always say when he was done. He'd then walk over and wrap his arm around her and pull her in for a kiss.

Besides the occasional frown, my mother would give him when he told that story, it was rare to see my parents argue. If they did disagree, they would partake in what they called enlightening debates. Their voices never raised, but sometimes a huff would escape from one or both their mouths as they bantered back and forth. I strived for a love like my parents...someday, but I wasn't necessarily focused on finding the one. I'd dated a guy name Tony for two years in high school, but he was a year ahead of me. When he went to college up in Maine, we tried to make it work. After three months apart, it fizzled. We called it quits.

Then there was Luke my sophomore year of college. I adored him. We met through a mutual friend who was a theater major. He was hardcore into the off-Broadway world and quite a bit older than me. He landed a lead role for a musical out in California and well, I have never been a west coast girl. New York is my home. I hear he's doing well though. The internet tells me. Luke was the last of my romances, so it's been a while since my mom has been able to swoon over a guy I was dating and since my sister has been with Trent for pretty much ever, I think she needed Drake, or at least the idea of Drake, to gush over.

"Well, I don't want to keep you from your *work thing*." I rolled my eyes at her air quotes. "I think I'm going to head to the store and get the grocery shopping in while it's quiet. You have fun!" She left me standing in the dining room alone. I followed only after I heard the door to her bedroom close at the end of the hall.

I took a quick shower to wash the hard work of the morning off me. My hair was still damp when one forty-five came around so, I wrapped it on top of my head and secured it with a few bobby pins before drawing eyeliner over my lash line and filling them in with some mascara. Okay, I added a bit of eyeshadow too. I figured I'd spice things up a bit. I may have been mortified with my mom poking around into my love life, but I wasn't blind. Drake was cute and even if I was only around for another few days, it was kind of nice to have him as a distraction.

11

Drake

Addie was not the type of girl that usually got under my skin. She was soft-spoken, a dreamer, and unafraid to try something new. I was taken aback by the way she erased all my surroundings the night before when we were talking. She would tip her head back when she laughed and I became entranced in the smile that followed. That same smile carried into my sleep last night and I impatiently waited for her to walk through the door that Sunday afternoon.

I used half the tables in the coffeehouse for the photoshoot set up. One of them was filled with three different kinds of brownies and another held multiple stacks of peanut butter, lemon shortbread, and coconut caramel cookies. My special gingerbread cookies were stacked on a table all their own. I shuttered at the amount of coffee we'd be pouring down the drain when this was over, but in the wake of that feeling, I admired the pristine artwork I had created. The foam atop each cup made shapes of hearts and leaves, and I'd even managed to work up the perfect winter snowflake with the flick of my wrist.

Mave was back in the kitchen cleaning up from the busy rush of the morning we had. She was cleaning much slower than usual. I think I even caught her cleaning a couple of the same areas twice. When I called her on it, she gave me a snarky response. "You mind your business now," she said. "I'll handle things back here my way. You just go do your thing with Ms. Addie." I raised my hands in defeat, but the wink she gave me before I turned around didn't go unnoticed.

I was sitting at the croissant table when Addie appeared through the window. Strands of hair blew across her face as she turned to grab the door handle. I've been in this town about a year now and although I loved the tight-knit community and that everyone knew my name within the first week, it always kind of felt as if it was missing something, or I guess someone. I realized that as my mind raced in bed the night before. Addie's smile was one thing that captivated me, but the extensive conversation and the comfort of being able to talk about my life and my dad, it came easy with her. It was something I hadn't found in Cold Spring. Not yet anyway.

A gust of frigid air followed Addie through the front door. She pulled off her tan hat. It was one of those with the big ball of fluff on top. My mom used to make me wear those when I was little and I'd never really understood the point in them. It was a constant punch in the head every time the ball flopped in a different direction. It looked good on her though.

"Hey there!" I waved over at her.

"Brrr," Addie said. She hugged her arms around herself and the sound of her boots shuffling across the floor echoed through the empty room. A trail of melted snow followed her closer to me. "The sun is deceiving." The pale pink painted on her cheeks was proof.

I let out a chuckle remembering the coldness of the snowflakes I walked through to get here this morning. "It was in the negatives last night. It's like the island tropics out there now." Her lips parted and a laugh escaped.

Winter in New York is a season no one ever gets used to. I have spent my whole life here in upstate and I still curse every time I have to scrape off my windshield or smack the ice from the corners of my door just to get inside. I wouldn't change it for anything though. If you're ever lucky enough to see the Hudson Valley in the summertime and how the marigold hues run into the crimson on the trees in the fall, you'd know why. I endured the harshness of winter frost because of the majestic rewards in the seasons that followed.

"After this, you'll find me in front of the fireplace for the rest of the day," Addie said.

"Ah man, I'm jealous. My place doesn't have one of those," I said.

I wasn't looking for an invitation, but the way her eyes darted away from mine made me think she took it that way. I forgot that the two of us weren't the only ones in the building until Mave popped up behind the counter.

"You could always go with her you know," Mave said. I jerked my head. She had come out of nowhere. Her elbows were now resting on the counter. "The B&B is always up for new visitors." She said with a continuous flicker of her brows.

"Ah, that's right." I knew all about the Church Street Bed and Breakfast. I passed by it on the days I walked down to the riverfront or the rare times I would hop the train to the city. I joked with Victoria when she first introduced herself about how a girl named Victoria grew up in a quaint Victorian. It was only last night when I put it together that Addie grew up in that home too. That's when I realized the depth of what Mave couldn't say out loud. I'd heard the talk around town about what a great man Gregory Pine was and what he had done for this town. I was in the local hardware store, maybe a month into my residency here in Cold Spring, when I learned what happened to him. I brought it up to Mave once, but all she said was that it was sad and that his wife and daughters were holding up the best they could.

I was aware of Victoria, but only last night did I realize the plural in daughters meant Addie too.

I watched Addie's head snap in Mave's direction. She mouthed something over at her, but I couldn't make it out. Her embarrassment was evident in the way her eyes flinched, so I tried to help her out by changing the subject.

"Are you ready to get started?" I asked. "I have everything set up, but feel free to fix it however you'd like."

"Great!" Addie said. She bent down and pulled the strap of the black bag off her shoulder and gently slide her camera from it. She took it into her hands and with a few adjustments of the lens, Addie was ready to go.

I didn't do too much as she worked. I stood back and watched her hands push plates in all different directions. She'd nod once they were where she wanted them and then a flood of clicking filled the room. "Can you do me a favor?" She pulled the camera from her face and turned to me. "Can you grab me those vases over there?"

She pointed to the long cement top bar that lined the window to the left of the front door. About a half dozen tiny white vases alternated with the napkin holders. Inside each of them were herbs from Mave's garden. I skipped over, snatched them up, and set them down on the table in front of her.

"Perfect! Stay right there." I froze where I was. Her weight fell on my shoulder as she pushed herself off the floor and onto one of the chairs. Her brown eyes usually came to right above my chest, but now I was looking up at them as she hovered over the table. I reached my hands out in preparation in case she lost her balance. "This is so much fun!" Her voice rose as she alternated between squatting down and standing back up on the chair.

I tried to ignore my pounding heart. Her unsteadiness was freaking me out. I squinted each time she came toward me, wondering if that was going to be the time she lost it and came barreling down on me. I could only hope my reflexes would be enough to catch her so that only I hit the white tile floor, but thankfully, I didn't have to find out.

After a few more clicks of the camera, Addie grabbed my hand and stepped off the chair. My pulse seemed to steady once she walked over to the table where the coffee sat. Her eyes were locked into the frame as she scrolled through the images.

"Let me see what you've got so far." I leaned over to peek, but she pulled away from me.

"No way!" I have to pick out the good ones and edit them first. Then I'll show you." I pushed out my bottom lip and let the corner of my eyes droop. "I promise. When they're ready, I'll show you."

"Alright," I groveled. "What's next?"

Addie tapped her finger to her chin then looked over at me with a smirk. I didn't know her that well yet, but I knew that kind of smirk. I'd seen it on a few of my exes. It came across right before they asked me for something they knew I wasn't going to offer up willingly. It worked backed then and it definitely worked for Addie.

"Sit here."

She pulled out the white chair in front of her. I shook my head, but that soft smile once again lured me in. I dragged my feet over and sunk into the chair. I had no idea what she had planned, but I sat there waiting, watching the wheels turning in her mind.

12

Addie

The coffee was a little too far to the left. Drake's shoulder was blocking it. I was in full photographer mode at that point that I hadn't realized my impulse to reach over his shoulder. My arm brushed against him as I wrapped my hand around the mug and pulled it further from where his arm rested. The warmth of his breath on my ear snapped me out of the trance I was in. I looked over to see his lips only inches from mine. Our stares hung in midair. He half-smiled and I watched his hazel eyes break from mine. They were now staring at my lips that hovered close to his.

"Ahem." A gurgled cough rang out from behind me and I shot myself back up. Both Drake and I flung our heads around to where Mave was standing. There was a sly grin across her lips. Her whole body was leaning to one side as her hand rested on her hip. "How's it going out here?" Mave asked.

I adjusted the collar of my coral sweater as my eyes plead with Mave not to make a big deal of this. I had a moment with a good-looking guy. It was a very small, fleeting moment where I happened to wonder what it may be like to kiss his lips, to welcome them in to dance with mine, but thanks to Mave that moment disappeared as fast as it came. Drake was now nervously strumming his fingers on the table next to the plate of croissants while I came to our rescue.

"It's going great," I said. I felt my hands press firmly against my camera to keep the shiver rising inside of me at bay. "I'm capturing some great stuff."

Mave couldn't help herself. She cut the tension in the room with her comic relief. "Yes, it sure looks like it from where I'm standing." I rolled my eyes and before the embarrassment became evident on my cheeks I stepped back and pressed the camera up to my face.

Click.

"I wasn't ready!" Mave yelled as her blue eyes flew wide. Her hands grabbed at her pin-straight ponytail.

"I know," I laughed. "It's called being candid." I pursed my lips and threw her an affectionate stare before getting back to work. "Alright," I said to Drake. "Grab the handle of that mug with that hand and hold a croissant in the other.

Drake's face fell as he realized what I was doing. This was a low-cost shoot. Technically, it was a no-cost shoot and I was using what I had. That included the catering manager. I pulled myself up onto one of the wobbly white chairs again.

"Watch yourself," Drake said. He let go of the coffee cup to still the movement of the chair with his palm. I looked down at his furrowed brows and smiled. His attentive nature towards me was appealing. I liked to think his need to keep me safe was because he cared. Of course, it also could have been that he didn't want a lawsuit on his hands if I fell and hurt myself inside the coffeehouse.

"I'm good," I said. I was standing steadily over him peering into the lens. "Get your hand back on that mug."

I heard Mave laugh softly behind us, but I was too busy lining up the perfect shot to acknowledge her. The natural light hit perfectly against the tops of the wood tables. Every ripple of the white leaf resting on top of the coffee stood out.

Click, click, click.

I leaned further over Drake and then bent down beside him. I repeated this like my own personal choreographed dance routine until I was sure I'd had enough content to work with. Drake was a trooper. He held his picturesque pose without wavering until I finally told him I was done.

"Oh, thank goodness," he said. His hands dropped to the table and he rolled out his shoulders. "I wasn't sure my muscles could hold me up any longer."

I could see the definition of his shoulder blades peeking out from underneath his chef coat. They looked strong enough to have been able to hold it for at least another five minutes, but I wasn't going to tell him that. While Drake shook out his arms, I looked over at Mave. She was organizing the muffins that were underneath the glass of the cake stand. Her blue blouse matched the specks of blueberries that were baked into them.

Click.

I took another candid...and then another. Finally, Mave noticed.

"Adelynne Dawn Pine." Her voice was sharp as she looked up to me with narrow eyes. Yes, that's the kind of town that I live in. Even those outside of my family know my full name and use it when they feel it's necessary.

"What?" I smirked. "I'm telling you; these kinds of photos are the best. They would be great for your website."

"Website? We don't have a website." Mave waved off my idea with the towel she used to clean the countertop.

"You don't?" My eyes pinned in her direction. This was the twenty-first century. How on earth could Mave's Coffeehouse not have a website? "How do people see your menu or put in takeout orders?"

"Oh, you two..." she wagged her finger at both us, "you're like two peas in a pod. They don't need a website. All they need to do is walk in," Mave said. She tossed the towel onto the counter and ran her fingers through her hair.

I looked down at Drake. He gave me the side-eye and then shrugged his shoulders. I knew that look. It was one of defeat. I'd known Mave long enough. She was set in her ways. A website was probably one of the many ideas Drake walked in here with but had yet to convince her was worth the effort. Mave yanked the tie that was holding her hair into place and her auburn hair fell across her shoulders. I could tell by the way her face now matched her hair color that she didn't want to have this conversation. "Are you kids done with these over here?" I nodded and she walked over to scoop up the plates of brownies.

I took some more photos of the pastries, the gingerbread cookies, and coffee Drake had set out before taking a few of the actual coffeehouse itself. After twenty minutes of watching Mave mope around with heavy footsteps across the floor, I decided to call it a day. I packed up my camera and walked over to Mave. She was viciously scrubbing the already spotless table in the corner. Either that table had done something to offend her or something was really wrong. I wanted to ask her but feared she'd transfer that intensity on to me.

"I'll see you tomorrow," I said. "I'll probably stop by sometime in the afternoon for a midday pick me up."

"Okay, sweetheart." Mave's hand came to a stop long enough to pull me in for a hug. "Take those gingerbread cookies with you when you go. No need for them to go to waste." I nodded, and once I walked away, she was back at it again.

I piled some of the gingerbread cookies into a paper bag and gathered up my things. Drake was standing near the door and pushed it open when I was close enough. The sun was a bit warmer now, but I could still feel the cold air blow across my nose. He stepped outside with me. I looked down at his once calm lips. They were shaking. I didn't want to torture him by keeping him outside, but I was worried about Mave.

"Is she okay?" I asked him. I shoved my hands into the pocket of my coat. Drake bowed his head and his eyes were now fixated on the indentations his shoes were making in the snow. His lips were still quivering, but that's not what stood out. It was his eyes. The way they burrowed themselves in every direction except for mine. "Drake, what's going on?"

"Nothing," he answered. "With the holidays and all, I think Mave is a little overwhelmed. That's all."

"Are you sure?"

His answer was vague, but the hollowness in his eyes made me refuse to believe it. He didn't give in. A gust of wind blew through the space that was between us and Drake's hand swiftly rubbed over his arm. The quivering from his lips was now taking over his whole body.

"I'm sure," he said. I wanted to believe him, but I knew it was a ploy. The way he shifted from side to side was my sign. I stopped digging so that he could walk back inside to the warmth and didn't freeze to death.

13

Addie

"Oh no! That is terrible!"

My eyes widened as I heard my mother's voice carry through the front door of the B&B as I walked inside.

She was standing behind the front desk with her back to me. I was careful not to slam the door once I was in the foyer. I didn't want to startle her, but I also didn't want to miss any part of what seemed like an interesting conversation.

"I understand," Mom said. "Don't you worry. We'll figure something out. You focus on getting better. Alright, dear. Bye-bye."

She hung the receiver over the black rotary style phone she's never been able to part with and let out a big sigh. I tiptoed closer to her and set my purse on the counter. It must have been all those years of sneaking in late in high school that made me so good at it. She had no idea I was there until the metal of my keys hit the counter. Her hands flew up and she spun her whole body towards me.

"Adelynne!" Her hands hit her chest. "You scared me."

"Sorry," I said. I couldn't help but smile though at the look that was still frozen on her face. Her eyebrows lifted and her mouth hung open. I waited until her breathing steadied before I butted in. "What was that all about?" I pointed at the phone.

"You remember Jennifer Wyatt, right?"

I nodded. Of course, I remembered Jennifer. She was one of only two regular babysitters I had growing up. She was also the elf that took pictures every year at our "Cookies with Santa" event. She'd showed up every year in a green dress, red tights, and black shoes that curled at the toes. The bell on her red and white striped hat would flop from side to side as she tried to get the perfect angle. Jennifer's love of the camera was one of the reasons I became interested in photography. I nodded at my mother's question as she continued.

"Well, the poor thing went ice skating after the festival and broke her ankle."

"Gosh, that is awful," I said.

"She doesn't think she'll be able to take pictures on Christmas Eve. I don't know how I'm going to find a photographer so last minute."

Her fingers twisted the softness of her brown hair. Her nose scrunched above her pursed lips as she thought hard. I looked over into the living room at the red velvet chair, thinking of all the times I sat upon Santa's lap. I was four the first year I jumped up without the help of my dad. As I grew older, I remember standing back and watching the glistening in the eyes of all the other children who followed in my footsteps. "Cookies with Santa" was one of the many traditions this town looked forward to every year. If Jennifer couldn't do it, I knew someone that would.

"Well," I said. "I know I'm not a professional, but I can try my hand at it."

"Really?" My mom's eyes lit up.

"Sure. Anything I can do go help. It'll be fun."

"Oh, Addie!" My mom said throwing her arms around me. "Thank you."

She didn't have to thank me. I was her daughter. This B&B was home. Christmas in Cold Spring was nothing without "Cookies with Santa."

"I'm happy to help," I said. Her grip was still tight around me.

"I'm so glad to hear you say that," she said.

Uh oh. That was all I could think. There was more. I knew it from the high-pitched sound of her voice in my ear. I slipped from her grasp and lifted my brows in anticipation of what she was about to say.

"Your sister should be here in about an hour. We're going to decorate the tree. Three and a half pairs of hands would be better than two."

"Three and a half?"

"Dylan," she winked. I smiled as I thought about my nephew. This was his first Christmas and I was so thankful I found the courage to be home for it. Making memories with him has shined a light over the darkness of losing my dad.

"I wouldn't miss it," I said.

"Great! Now, come help me pull the ornaments from the attic."

"Ah, there's the catch. No one said anything about manual labor." I laughed. So did my mom as I followed her up the stairs.

It took every bit of the hour until Victoria arrived to dig through the attic and find the boxes of ornaments for the tree. Some of them were hidden underneath the Fourth of July decorations. Others were mixed with Valentine's décor. After all these years, the attic probably could use a makeover, but that was a story for another time. I was halfway down the stairs with the final box of ornaments when Victoria arrived.

"We're here!" She yelled from the foyer.

"In here," my mom shouted from the living room.

I saw her with Dylan in her arms as I stepped slowly. The box was heavier than I thought it was. I was out of breath when I got there, but I made it to the living room.

"Hey little guy," I said before bending down to relieve myself from the wait of the box. Dylan's blue eyes stared widely at me. His little lips quivered, and I expected a loud wail to follow, but it never did. I knew it was safe to reach out my hands when a faint smile crossed his face. "Come here."

I pulled him from Victoria's arms and pressed the softness of his cold cheek against mine. I was naïve when it came to the stealth of a two-month-old. As I snuggled Dylan in his fuzzy baby blue, footed pajamas against my chest, he was gripping his tiny little fingers around the tips of my hair. It wasn't until he began to wiggle in my arms that I felt the pain at my roots. I opened my mouth, but nothing came out at first. That was until he pulled again.

"Ouch!" My hand flew up to meet his and Victoria, in a fit of laughter, tried to help. It took both of us to pry Dylan's fingers open and free my hair. A baby vs. two grown women and he almost won. It was as if he knew what he was doing because once my hair was free from his grasp, I swear he let out a chuckle.

"I should have warned you about that," Victoria said as she reached down to open the boxes. "He's been doing that a lot lately. Can you believe how strong he is already?"

"I wouldn't have five minutes ago, but now I don't doubt it," I said.

I was prepared when Dylan's tiny fingers reached for my nose. This time, I turned his back to me and distracted him with the ornaments in Victoria's hands.

"You want to do the honors?" Victoria asked. I looked over at her as she held out the elf ornament with my dad's name on it.

"Are you sure?" I asked. She nodded.

I looked over at my mom and knew by the way her eyes glistened that she agreed. I took the ornament from Victoria's hand and searched the tree for the perfect branch to set my dad's ornament. When I found one on the side closest to the fireplace, instead of placing it there myself, I let Dylan help. He wrapped his hand around my finger, I lifted his arm up to the branch and slipped the thin white string around the pine needles. I don't think I can describe the way I felt watching Dylan stare at the ornament as it swayed to a stop. His mouth open and his eyes so wide I could see the twinkle of the tree lights in them.

"Was that fun?" I asked him. Victoria reached out another ornament to me. This time, my name was on it. I let Dylan grab my finger again and I slipped the ornament a few branches below my father's. I saved the branch next to his for my mother's ornament.

Dylan helped me put a few more ornaments on the tree before he became restless. That's when Victoria set him on a blanket underneath hanging circus animals. That's where he stayed until my mother, Victoria and I were done flooding the tree with all of our memories. Once the boxes were empty, we stepped back to admire our hard work.

"It's beautiful," Victoria said.

"It sure is," I chimed in.

"Dad would love it." Mom chimed in.

We all looked at each other and nodded. My dad would have been proud.

14

Drake

I took a deep breath as I stood on the sidewalk staring at the wooden door in front of me. I knew if I walked through it, I could possibly lose my job. If I didn't, if I turned around and walked away, any chance I had of saving my job would leave with me. I gave myself a pep talk and by the time I convinced myself that this was for the best, that door had opened and out came Victoria.

"Drake? What are you doing here?" Her eyes widened as she looked down at me from the porch.

"Hey!" I picked up my feet and walked up the stairs to stand beside her. "

A pink scarf draped across the front of her oversized navy coat. She tilted her head as she readjusted her grip on the baby carrier in her hands. Dylan's eyes were staring widely at me. I tickled the green blanket that lay over him and he let out a soft cooing noise. I looked back up at Victoria.

"I was wondering if Addie was here by chance."

"She sure is! Come on inside. I'll get her." Victoria waved me in. I watched Dylan's eyes flicker as she flung the carrier around to move back inside. "Mom, Drake is here to see Addie."

"Hello, Mrs. Pine."

"Oh honey, please, call me Becky," she said.

I can't even remember how many times that woman has told me to call her by her first name. I tried sometimes, but then my mother's voice would creep into my head. It was proper to refer to a lady by their surname. I nodded as I pulled the hat from my head and gripped it tightly in my hand. I could feel both Becky and Victoria's tapered stare on my face, but I offered them no explanation of why I was there.

"I'll run and grab her," Becky said leaving me alone with an inquisitive Victoria.

"I take it Addie didn't scare you off the other night seeing that you're here," she joked.

"Not at all. She's really great."

I was afraid of where this conversation was going, but right as Victoria was about to open her mouth to say something else, a tiny ball of brown fur lunged at my leg. I felt the sharpness of its nails in my shin as I bent down to pet it.

"Hudson, no jump!" I looked up to find Addie standing in the hallway. Her waves of brown hair were nestled in a lopsided bun and her hand peeked out enough from her baggy blue and white striped sweater to scorn the dog she left me for the other night. Addie marched over and bent down to my level. "I'm so sorry. We're still learning." She reached out to pull the squirmy pup away from me.

"It's no problem. I like dogs." I did really like dogs. I grew up on six acres. That was plenty of room for the three that we always had at one time. They were all much bigger than Hudson. He would've probably gotten lost in the overgrown weeds and mature trees that lined our property.

Hudson flopped his head over Addie's shoulder and I couldn't help but smile as she started to sway back and forth with him in her arms. I was so focused on the way Addie's head folded against the dog that I had yet to notice I now had three pairs of eyes staring at me.

"So, what's up?" Addie asked. My eyes bounced back and forth between her, Victoria, and Becky. I'm not sure if it was the way my hands were drumming the sides of my legs or the way the complexion drained from my face, but I'm glad that Addie picked up on at least one of them. "Here, let's go sit in the living room."

Addie bent down and released her grip on Hudson who ran into the direction we were heading. When I turned the corner into the living room Hudson was already on the couch. His stub of a tail trying so hard to show his excitement and his front paws bounced against the tan colored pillow.

"I'm sorry to barge in like this," I said sitting myself down next to Hudson. His wet tongue found my chin immediately. I let him get in a couple of licks before I pulled him onto my lap and started rubbing his belly.

"It's totally fine," Addie said. I was sitting out on the screened porch listening to a crime podcast. They're addicting and completely unproductive. I'm happy for the distraction." She let a quiet chuckle slip from her lips and patted Hudson's head.

Crime podcasts weren't necessarily my forte, but when it came to being completely consumed in a futile activity, I was right there with her. There was a cutlery store up in Rhinebeck where I could spend hours sifting through gadgets and baked goods. I did spend hours there when I went to the CIA. Now that it was a good hour drive away it had turned into a day trip activity. Two hours to drive and a few more to browse. That wasn't really important as the two of us sat across from each other. I had come on a mission.

"I wanted to talk to you about the other day. You know when you mentioned the website and Mave went all *redrum* on you as if she was the star of *The Shining?*" Addie nodded. "Well, I think I'm going to need your expertise, but we may have to keep it on the down-low.

Addie readjusted her lopsided bun. It was a little more centered now but still leaned to the right. "I think I kind of like where this is going, but I'm going to let you finish before I decide," she said.

I knew this part was going to be hard for Addie to hear. It would be even harder to hear it from someone she barely knew, but telling her was my only hope. "Well, the coffeehouse...we're struggling a bit." That was an understatement. We were months behind in rent and the landlord was threatening to end our lease if we couldn't come up with the money soon. He had already allowed a few months to slide, but he couldn't do it much longer. After decades of sitting on Main Street, Mave's was in jeopardy.

"What do you mean struggling?" Addie leaned in further toward me and my chest fell heavy as I watched the concern in her eyes grow.

"Mave's behind on paying some of her bills. With the expansion of the menu, we've been able to close the gap some. We can keep the lights on, but with the new restaurants and other coffeehouses opening in town, the competition has taken its toll."

I hated the way the corners of Addie's lips dropped. She stood up from the couch and folded her arms together. I heard the thud as they slammed into her chest. The knots in my stomach pulled at me harder.

"Are you telling me we might lose Mave's Coffeehouse?" Addie whimpered. I sat silent. "No! No, that can't happen!" I set Hudson back down on the pillow next to me and used whatever ounce of strength I could find to stand myself up. I could see the sadness building up in Addie's eyes as I walked toward her. I tried to offer comfort by gripping my hands around her shoulders. "That coffeehouse is all Mave has." Her glassy brown eyes looked up at me. "It's been a part of this town since forever. We can't lose it."

Addie fell into my chest before I could see the tears fall. I wrapped my arms around her and rubbed my hands along her back. Guilt rose inside of me. I hated that I had been the one to make her cry, but I was also relieved that I was no longer the only one carrying this secret. I let Addie's head rest against me while she quietly sobbed. When she was done, she pulled herself away and rubbed the wetness from her cheeks.

"What do we have to do? How can I help? I'll do anything," she said.

"Well, you know as well as I do that this town gets its business from the tourists. People need to see the menu and daily specials and the whole ordering online, that was a great idea."

"Yeah! Especially for those who come to hike Breakneck or visit the Foundry. Not everyone comes to make a day of shopping and hanging out at the Riverfront. They want something quick to grab and eat on the train." Her face lit up as she went on. "I'm amateur, but I think I can work something up. I can put something together pretty quickly and once it's live we can always tweak it from there."

She slapped her palms together and I was relieved to see that a smile had replaced her sadness. For the past year, I've tried to get Mave to agree to a website, but she so badly wanted to believe that the small-town charm would reel people in. I wholeheartedly believe that it would, but they had to know we existed first. The sign outside was no longer enough to fill the tables. I didn't waste any more of Addie's time. We didn't have a lot left to try and turn this around.

"Thank you," she said, "for telling me and for letting me help."

"Of course." Addie walked me to the front door and followed me out onto the porch. "Here's my number. If you need anything from me, let me know."

"I will, thanks Drake."

"Thank you, Addie." Her smile was the last thing I saw before I turned around. I think it was that moment that changed everything for me. When I first met Addie, I thought she was cute. The night at the festival, when we sat on the bench talking, I thought she was funny and smart, but today was different. I loved what I did and I sacrificed a lot to do it. My relationship with my father was on the mend, but I don't know if it would ever be the same. I didn't want to lose this job. I loved working with Mave and I had fallen in love with Cold Spring. This was where I was meant to be. I strolled through the wetness of the street away from the bed and breakfast. Addie's smile still clouded my mind. She was more to me now than a girl I was attracted to. Addie Pine was the girl who restored my hope.

15
Addie

There was no way that I was going to let Mave's Coffeehouse shut its doors. I was not going to walk down Main Street and look through those glass windows to see a clothing store or big money restaurant that some stranger looking to make a buck waltzed into town and put in. That's why I loved Cold Spring so much. We didn't have chain stores. We had small businesses with family history.

I jotted down a few ideas in a notebook for the website and I wanted to get started on it right away, but I needed to help my mom set up for dinner first. Three rooms were occupied in this B&B and there were a few additional dinner reservations in the books for tonight. I was hiding out in the dining room trying to escape Victoria's endless questions about Drake. I gave him my word I wouldn't say anything about the trouble Mave was in, but that wasn't what she wanted to know. I could see the snarky look in her eyes when Drake left. It was all too familiar. She used to look at me that way in high school right before breaking out into the teasing repetition of Addie and, *insert boy name here*, sitting in a tree. I knew I couldn't hide for long. I was setting the silverware in the dining room when Victoria and my mother came in with plates and glassware in their hands. I braced myself.

"You know, we'll probably have a spot or two open tonight if Drake wants to join us for dinner," Victoria said. I felt my lips tighten, but I refused to look in her direction.

"I'm sure he has more important things to do," I said. I think the forks in my right hand were starting to feel my wrath as I strengthened my grip around them.

"Did you even ask?"

"No, Victoria." I deliberately pressed the fork into the napkin on the table.

"Tori darling, leave your sister alone. If she doesn't want to share her personal life with us, she's not obligated."

Tori darling, leave your sister alone. Man, do I remember those words on repeat growing up. I love my sister, but like any older sibling, she really knows how to get under my skin. Whether it was stealing toys or fighting over which morning cartoon to watch, we had the bickering down to science growing up. Being home was a reminder that we might have been older, but sibling rivalry never fades.

"Why don't you go grab the lilies from the foyer for the centerpieces," Mom said. Victoria nodded and disappeared through the open archway for a moment before returning with a handful of calla lilies.

"You know, I went to go visit dad the other day," Victoria said. "There was a bouquet of these lying in front of his headstone."

I was at the last place setting. My hand pressing the spoon firmly onto the table and I couldn't let go. My hands froze at Victoria's words. It wasn't that I was hiding my visit to the cemetery. It'd been three years since I'd come home. None of us had talked about what happened. I bottled it up and threw myself into New York City life. It'd only been two days since I came home, and I wasn't sure where any of us were when it came to talking about him.

"That's lovely." A smile grazed my mother's face. "They were his favorite for these centerpieces. Every few days he'd head over to Millie's to replace the ones that were wilting. Did I ever tell you the story about why they became his flower of choice?"

I looked over at my mother. The bits of silver that intertwined through her brown hair illuminated from the recessed lights above. Her blue and white floral dress flowed as she walked over to pull out one of the chairs tucked under the table. She sunk into it and pulled out two other chairs across from her. With both hands, she patted the seat cushions. I followed Victoria over and we sat down in front of her.

"The very first time I brought your father up here to meet your grandparents, we went to the drive-in theater up in Poughkeepsie. We borrowed your grandfather's convertible and drove up Route 9 in the middle of the July heat. The air conditioning was broken and before the movie even started, I was in tears at how the humidity stole the curls out of my hair and left a trail of black mascara down my face."

I let out a soft laugh and Victoria dropped her face to her hands. It was so vivid in my mind. We'd gone to that movie theater many times growing up and I was only now hearing this story."

"It's funny to look back on," Mom said, "but at that moment I was devastated. Your father excused himself from the driver's seat and I thought 'this is it; we're going back to college and he'll never talk to me again.' After ten minutes he returned to the car with a bucket of popcorn, two sodas, and a calla lily."

My mother pulled one of the calla lilies from Victoria's grasp. She massaged the stem with her fingers and I watched the ivory petals float around in circles. Her eyes grew wide and along with her smile as she too stared at the movement. After a deep inhale of its floral scent, she started the story again.

"He handed me the calla lily and asked if I knew what it symbolized. I shook my head. 'Beauty,' he said. 'And humidity hair or not there's no one more beautiful than you.'"

My father always had a way of making any bad situation better. The calla lily story didn't surprise me. It reminded me of my senior ball. I went with a boy named Matthew. He was a part of the swim club in Poughkeepsie. I had to get a permission slip signed to bring someone who wasn't from our school. I didn't like him like that, but I liked him enough to take him to the ball. Our feet were hanging off the diving boards one night after practice and we started talking about our respective dances. He didn't have a date to his either. So, with our toes grazing over the chlorine-filled water, we made a pact. We'd go together to both.

Mine was two weeks before his. He stepped out of his blue sedan and walked up the steps with a brown box clutched tight in his hand. When he opened it, a wilted pink rose rested inside. Turns out, he picked up the corsage the night before and left it in the trunk of his car. It had been at least mid-eighties all week. That rose didn't stand a chance. My father could see the embarrassment in the way Matthew's head bowed to the floor. Without hesitation, he ran out to the back garden and walked back in with purple lilacs. *"These will match better anyway,"* my father said. He handed the lilacs to my mother who maneuvered the pin through the stems and secured it onto my pale-yellow dress. Just like I imagined my mother did in the car the night he told her that her humidity hair was beautiful, Matthew smiled. Two weeks later he made sure he placed the box in his refrigerator before I arrived at his house.

I felt a coldness on my cheek thinking back to that moment. I wiped my hand across the smoothness of my damp skin. My mother set the calla lily on the table and leaned over to me.

"Don't cry sweet girl," she said. She slid her chair closer and pulled me into the warmth of her embrace. That only made the stream of tears fall steadier.

"I'm so sorry," I was able to mumble through the saltiness of my lips. "I should've come home more."

The guilt I was suddenly feeling for my lack of attendance these past few years was pounding at my chest like a hammer. My slow breaths had turned into loud sobs. The heaving was so piercing that the words coming from my mother's mouth to try to calm me failed.

"No, you listen to me, both of you." My mother leaned back and gripped my head in her hands. "You lost your father. It was sudden and it hurt. There is no right or wrong way to deal with a tragedy like that. Healing comes on our own time and in our own way."

"You're here now and that's what matters," Victoria intervened. She pressed the palm of her hand against my back.

They were right. We all handled our grief differently. My mother threw herself even more into the B&B with renovations. Victoria and Trent took a bucket list trip to Thailand and I hibernated in the city that never sleeps. It took three years, but I was back now, and to be honest, my heart was happier in these last few days than any time over the years of my denial. I loved being back in the daily grind of the B&B. I loved seeing Dylan and Victoria regularly and now, with my new task to help save Mave's Coffeehouse, there was a sense of belonging flowing through me that I hadn't felt since my father died.

I pushed myself up from the chair and brushed the tear-soaked hair from my face. "It's good to be home," I said. "Now, let's get some dinner started!" I clapped my hands out in front of me and my mother and Victoria both joined in with my laughter. It was a noise I hadn't heard in so long that I had almost forgotten how magical it sounded. We were my father's three musketeers and we were finally together again.

I was feeling invigorated after my talk with Mom and Victoria. All through dinner I was thinking of ways to help Mave and the new website design she would hopefully adopt. I barely ate because I too antsy and wanted to dive into the work. Once the dinner guests had retreated back to their rooms, I did the same. I flipped open my laptop and scrolled through all the photos I had taken during the photoshoot at Mave's. I picked the best ones, edited them, and placed them in the website layout.

By the time it came to write out all the different sections like *history, menu, about us,* and all the other grand things a website can't do without, my stomach was growling. I placed my hand over it and immediately regretted not finishing my chicken cordon bleu. Within reach was the box of cookies that Mave made me take home from the coffeehouse. A sugar rush would be the perfect way to satisfy my aching stomach and give me a little push to get this website done as fast as I could. Mave needed help now.

I flipped the top of the cardboard box open and was met with the aroma of gingerbread. Each one was perfectly decorated with red and green icing. They looked almost too good to eat. *Almost.* I snatched one up and the soft texture melted in my mouth.

"Oh my gosh," I mumbled. "These are so good." I inhaled the first cookie in fewer bites than I probably should have and picked up another. I savored the taste of cloves and fennel. My mother had been baking gingerbread cookies for decades and don't get me wrong, they were good enough for me to stash in my room at Christmas time, but these, these cookies were out of this world. They were right up there with the mouthwatering lemon tarts Drake introduced me to the day I first met him.

After I devoured the second cookie, I got an idea. One that was so good, I had to tell Drake. I pulled out my phone and sent him a text.

Addie: *Do you have plans tomorrow?*

It took a few minutes, but his response came.

Drake: *Nothing other than the usual. Free after 2.*

Addie: *Perfect!*

I devised a plan on when and where to meet. Once Drake confirmed, I got back to work. I couldn't wait to put this idea together. Hopefully, Drake would be on board with it because without him, I'd be out of luck and Mave would be out of business.

16

Drake

I was not expecting the town of Beacon to be as lively as it was when I swerved my car into a parallel spot on the street. It was a weekday, late in the afternoon, but it was the holiday season, so I should've known. Children were out of school and by the looks of it, they were using the sidewalks as their current playground. I thrust the car into park as I watched a young boy with a black hat and mittens to match skip along beside an older woman.

Behind them were dozens of other people walking in all directions. I stepped into the slush on the pavement, slammed the driver's side door and maneuvered my way through the crowd. It was Addie's idea to meet here. She was feeling a bit guilty about conspiring behind Mave's back, so she wanted to do it somewhere she knew we wouldn't get caught.

It'd been a while since I had ventured down to Beacon. It wasn't far from Cold Spring, only a ten-minute drive towards the city. Walking along Main Street, I was almost swept back in time. The heavy red-brick architecture surrounded me, but what once was an industrial city has now been revitalized with boutiques, bookstores, coffeehouses, distilleries, and more. Beacon was quickly trailing on the heels of Cold Spring as a retreat for city dwellers and with the abundance of storefronts I walked past, I could see why.

The streets were so crowded that I felt like the ball in a pinball machine as I made my way to the bread company Addie and I agreed to meet for a coffee. It had been snowing the last couple of days and not the pretty kind. It was the heavy, wet, too dense to build a snowman, kind of snow, but today seemed to have escaped it. Today, the sun was shining its warmth on the bareness of the trees that lined the streets. I felt a couple of drops on my head fall from one of the branches hanging over the door of the bread company as I opened it. *Please don't let there be a bird above my head.* That's all I could think as I swept my hand across the top of my head. I let out a heavy sigh when I pulled it back down to find remnants of only melted snow.

"You alright?" I heard a voice call out. Addie was already inside. The top part of her hair was clipped back away from her face. A thin layer of shimmer spread across her lips. I nodded as I took in the fluffy gray jacket and the purple rain boots that covered her black leggings.

"It's hopping here today," I said. Addie turned her head to the sea of bodies that filled every table in the tiny room.

"I know! I got here a little early and snagged us some seats in the back."

I followed the sound of Addie's boots to the back corner of the room. Her computer was set up on the wooden table along with two glasses of water. I don't know if it was the influx of people around us or if the heat was cranked up high in this place, but I could feel the fire on my face as I sat down. I yanked off my hat and unzipped my jacket. The waitress was at our table before I even flung my coat around the back of the chair. Once she left with our orders, Addie got right down to business.

"Okay, are you ready?" Addie asked.

She took my silence as a yes and slowly slid the computer screen to face me. The photos that Addie had taken of my baking creations were splattered across the screen below bold, black letters that read Mave's Coffeehouse. I smiled as she scrolled down the page. Halfway through, there I was in my chef's hat. I never was one for the spotlight, but it looks like I wasn't going to be able to hide from this thanks to Addie.

"Check this part out." Her voice rose as she clicked the big white button to reveal the menu. "All regular items are listed here and this over here," she pointed to the far right of the screen, "is where we can incorporate pick up orders."

"I like it!" I think I probably would've liked anything Addie had made at that point because I was starting to like Addie. I loved the way her eyes lit up talking about the bits and pieces of the site. I loved the way one side of her lip curled higher than the other as she smiled through her presentation. She had such a vision, and it came easy for her. Watching her scroll through the pages of detail made it evident that her talents were wasting away behind a desk in the city. "What's this?" I asked. A photo of my specially made gingerbread cookies just popped up over the screen.

"Oh, that..." Addie said. Her brows lifted, and I could see a mischievous glare in those sweet caramel eyes. "That is my genius idea." My eyes widened. She clicked the gingerbread photo and my jaw dropped. "I know it's short notice," she said, "but I think it'll be a great trial run for next year and a test for online ordering from the website."

The waitress had returned only for a moment to place down our coffee orders. I leaned forward to read a little more on the page. *Get your last-minute holiday orders today! Fresh out-of-the-oven and ready for pickup on December 23.*

December 23 was five days away. That's when my parents were coming to town. We were closing up the shop for the holidays in two days. I planned to spend this afternoon finishing up some Christmas shopping and then lounge around in my plaid pajama bottoms until my parents arrived and I would have to put on real clothes to show them I wasn't a complete bum here in the life they didn't approve of. I think Addie could tell by the way I squinted my eyes at the computer that I wasn't all in, yet anyway.

"I know, I know, it's Christmas, but I'll cap the order and once they're all baked, I'll take it from there. I'll wrap them up, tie them with a bow and be there during the pickup window to hand them out. Since most of the bakeries will close prior, this gives us an advantage."

Ah, the way her eyelashes were fluttering at me. How could I not say yes? I had a lot of gingerbread dough stuffed in the bakery freezer, so a few dozen orders wouldn't be all that hard.

"Alright," I said. "Let's do it."

"Yes!" Addie threw her hands up. My heart was pounding knowing that I was the reason for that sparkle in her eyes. She'd captivated me from the moment I met her, but sitting across the table with her waves of brown hair unraveling from her ponytail, she completely did me in. I was all in. Anything she needed from me, she was going to get it. Now, the two of us only had to hope that Addie could convince Mave. She was person who had the money to allow us to hit publish on this website. Hopefully she too would see that this was an opportunity we couldn't pass up.

"I have a little shopping to do before I head back. Want to join?" I asked.

Addie snapped her laptop closed. I watched as she wrapped her lips around her straw and took another long sip of her coffee. I didn't have to be a genius to know that she was stalling. I'd seen it many times before. It was the dreaded silence that came before the rejection.

"Where you headed? I might be interested," she said.

"To the local glass shop. My mom loves that kind of stuff and she's the last person I have to shop for. Have to get it wrapped before she gets here."

"Your parents are coming for the holidays?" Addie asked.

"Yeah. They haven't been to Cold Spring since I moved. I'm basically twisting their arms. They'd much rather be back in New Paltz, but this is my home now. I want them to fall in love with it the way I have."

I felt Addie's hand rest on my forearm. Her eyes looked longingly at me and I wondered if she felt sorry for me. My relationship with my parents wasn't storybook, but at least they were both here. I didn't want to undermine that for her, so I tried to change the subject.

"I've been making a list of all the fun things there are to do here. There really is a ton for a small town."

"There sure is!" Addie said. "The B&B does a Christmas Eve event every year. It's open to everyone. You should bring them. We decorate cookies and Santa comes." She looked up at me and winked. "You should start making a list for him."

I felt the temperature in my face rise again. Addie's carefree attitude was exactly what I needed these days. The only thing that stung was the idea of introducing Addie to my parents. It had the donut I ate before I got here doing backflips in my stomach. My mother, though I loved her, could be a bit brass and my father, well, the fact that I had barely spoken to him in the last couple years because of his feelings about the town Addie grew up in, that was enough to want to rescind the invitation. I looked up at her wide-eyed grin and watched her hands sweep her hair behind her ears. She was so delicate and sweet that it was seemingly impossible to disappoint her.

"That sounds fun. I'll talk to them about it when they get into town."

"Okay." Her smile grew wider. "Well then, since we have a lot of work to do, we better get shopping."

Addie slapped her palms together and I laughed as the table shook. A day of shopping meant I got to spend more time with her. It also meant I had someone with better taste to help me pick out my mother's present. After I insisted on taking care of the check, the two of us bundled up for the winter air and headed out onto the streets of Beacon.

17

Addie

"Are you nervous?" I asked. I knew Drake and his father didn't have the best history.

"About what?" Drake asked.

The two of us were clasping at the collars of our jackets trying to stop the ice-cold wind from hitting our skin. The breeze from the water was ferocious that morning. Even the sun couldn't stop the bite of the Hudson River.

"Your parents coming to town."

"Oh, that. I don't know," Drake said. "It's been tough the last few years being distant. My family was always close. There was never anything I couldn't tell my dad growing up and now any conversation we have seems to turn into an argument."

"I'm sorry."

Hearing about Drake's strained relationship with his dad made tears well up in my eyes. I knew how precious time was and how quickly it could be taken away. I wanted to shake Drake's father for letting something like his son's dream cause a rift between them. I missed my dad so much. Being back here in the Hudson Valley had this weird way of being torturous and therapeutic at the same time. I felt closer to my father, to my mother and my sister than ever before, yet it took his absence to bring us closer.

"I think once your dad sees your life here, he'll understand," I said. "And if not, he definitely will when he tastes those gingerbread cookies."

I looked over at Drake. The corners of his lips curled up slightly. He let out a quiet laugh. "Maybe," he said. "I probably wouldn't want to place a bet on it though. Anyway, tell me about your dad. From what I hear he was a pretty cool guy."

"He sure was," I said. Cars splashed through the usual wet mush that filled the streets after a snowstorm. I had to dodge the aftermath of flying slush twice before I could continue. "To be honest, Cold Spring wasn't his cup of tea at first either."

"Really?" Drake's eyes widened as he turned his head towards me and slowed his pace.

"Not at all. My dad loved New York City. It was never a thought in his mind that he would leave. He told me that it wasn't until he met my mom that his opinion changed. When he looked at her, he saw kids running around in a backyard full of green grass. He saw her standing on the sidewalk in a little neighborhood waiting for the school bus to arrive. His life went from hailing cabs to mowing lawns."

"Do you think he ever regretted it?" Drake asked.

"If he did, it never showed," I said. One of the things I was grateful for was that I could still remember my dad vividly every time I thought of him. I had this fear after the funeral that his face would fade from my mind and I would forget what he looked like, but as I talked to Drake about the man who made me, his balding head and oversized glasses came to view. "My dad was always smiling. He was always willing to lend a hand to anyone who needed it and that included Mave. That is why I can't bear to think of the coffeehouse not being here."

One year when I was maybe ten, an ice storm swept across the Hudson Valley and the roof caved in. Mave had just inherited the coffee shop and didn't even know where to start. When my dad and I walked in that day, she was hugging her knees on the floor against the counter. Her sobs resounding of the fear I'm sure she was feeling. My dad didn't hesitate. Once the power was back on, he was on the phone with the insurance company and started the process of replacing the roof and getting Mave's back into business as soon as he could.

"I hate that she's going through this," I said. The two of us took the final turn toward the glass shop. I could see the skinny, multi-story, brick building straight ahead. "I'm glad she has you though. You seem to balance her out by being the calm to her crazy."

"Haha! I think that's a perfect description of our partnership," Drake said.

He reached for the door handle and I stepped in front of him, underneath the chiming bell and into the bustling store. I loved the way the sun glistened through the tall windows illuminating each piece of blown glass that sat on the shelves.

"Gosh, it's been a minute since I've been here." I could hear my mother's voice in my head as I cautiously admired the selves of vases.

Don't touch.

I hovered over them to get a better look. There was one in every color from sea green to hues of yellows and oranges.

"What kind of stuff does your mom like?" I asked.

"She loves flowers and party planning," Drake said.

"So, these vases would be nice or... woah, look at that." My voice raised as my eyes came upon a gorgeous gold and blue wave bowl. It looked the same as it sounded. The crystal blue edges of the bowl reflected waves of the ocean and melted perfectly into the golden hues of the base.

"She'd love that!" Drake's eye widened almost as wide as the smile on his face.

"You think?" I asked.

"Definitely. Wow, you made this easy."

I could feel the heat in my cheeks, and I knew by the way Drake looked at me that it was obvious how much I appreciated those words. Drake carefully lifted the bowl from the shelf, and we walked to the front to check out. I watched the cashier fold pieces of brown paper around the bowl before slipping it into a sparkly red bag. Drake slipped his fingers through the handle and we both waved goodbye.

"Thanks again for coming with me," Drake said once we were back outside.

"Of course. Thanks for meeting me out here today and for agreeing to my crazy plan."

"I want to save Mave's as much as you do," he said. "Honestly, I'm glad I don't have to carry this secret by myself. Mave will kill me for telling you, but I'm happy I did."

"Me too," I said.

"You're easy to talk to. I know it's weird but, ever since you came around, my world kind of spins a little slower. I appreciate things a bit more."

I smiled. I knew what he meant. I felt the same way. That's why it was so easy when he stopped in the middle of that sidewalk and turned towards me. I looked up into his eyes, which today were more of a blue than green the way the sun was hitting them. He lifted the hand that wasn't holding the bag with the glass bowl to my cheek and the moment the leather of his gloves touched me, my heart began to race. It felt like the day of the photoshoot in the coffeehouse all over again, except this time, it wasn't me getting caught up in the moment. We were going to do this. Drake was going to kiss me. His head lowered. I closed my eyes and clenched my jacket hoping that when his lips touched mine, I didn't lose all control and fumble forward. The warmth of his breath was at my lips. I closed my eyes tighter and just as I started to feel the chill of his lips wrap over mine, a car came speeding by, and instead of falling into an embrace, the two of us were now covered in soggy snow. The water sopped across my face and I yanked myself back.

"Oh my gosh!" I yelped. "Are you serious?" I shook my arms violently, thinking that the water would miraculously slide off the cotton of my gray coat.

"Wow." That was the only word Drake could muster as he slid the back of his leather glove over his forehead. The two of us were now standing on Main Street in Beacon, soaking wet and laughing hysterically. There wasn't much else we could do, but secretly I hoped that wouldn't be the last attempt at a first kiss.□

18

Addie

I never knew how much of a thrill hitting the publish button would give me. I'd hit it many times at work, but I suppose knowing it was someone else's work took the fun out of it. Not this time though. Mave's Coffeehouse officially had a website and all the grit and intricate details were of my doing.

I clicked the refresh button once I crawled into bed that night. Hudson was snuggled up by my feet. By the soft putter he made with each breath, I knew he was fast asleep. I envied him. With every blink, my eyes were determined to stay closed, but I couldn't seem to move the computer from my lap even though the tiny little number underneath the word orders still read zero. I was disheartened because I thought the gingerbread cookies were a genius idea. It had only been six hours, a very long six hours. I'm surprised my fingertips weren't sore from how many times I'd pressed that same button on the right side of my computer.

It had taken all morning to convince Mave to let us make the site live. In the middle of bells ringing and customer's orders, Drake and I listed off every plus for the coffeehouse. For every good thing, she threw a bad one back at us. *Who's going to fix this website when something goes wrong? I don't have time to update it. The money could be better spent elsewhere.*

I assured Mave that I had the time to make changes to the website. That was the benefit of working in the basement. As long as my work got done, no one paid too much attention. I thought that may have worked when she paused with her hand on her hips, but when another customer walked up to the register, she simply rolled her eyes and walked away from me.

"Just give us to the new year. Let us get through the cookie orders. What can it hurt?" I asked.

I sat in my bed laughing as I thought about how pathetic I must have sounded to Mave that morning. I squeezed my palms together in front of my chest and pushed my bottom lip out toward her. "Please Mave." That did it. She gave in.

"Oh, thank you, thank you, thank you!" I threw my arms around her and slapped hands softly with Drake behind Mave's back. I could tell by the wink he gave me that we were on the same page. We'd revel in silence since we knew Mave was going against her better judgment on this one.

Drake and I agreed that we'd stock ten orders on the website. If that went well, then maybe we'd add another ten. It wasn't a whole lot of income, but the point was to get more people to the website and bring more customers into the store. They'd come to pick up their cookies, we'd give them a voucher for a free coffee. Since Mave's became a café, no one has ever been able to leave Mave's with only a cup of coffee. Upselling. That's what I learned in college. They come in for one thing and you convince them they also need something else. Baby steps. That's what we were doing here.

I tapped the button again one more time before I called it a night. Still zero. I shrugged, then placed the computer on my nightstand and hit the button on the lamp to make my room go dark.

"Maybe tomorrow," I said. My eyes were heavy. Hudson had stumbled up to the pillow next me and I patted his head before laying back. My head fell hard into my pillow. "Maybe tomorrow there will be an order." It was wishful thinking as I yawned and drifted off to sleep. Wishful thinking that was about to become more of a reality than I had anticipated.

*

Growing up in a bed and breakfast, the clanging of pans and dishes in the kitchen had become like meditation music to me. I'd become accustomed to sleeping through it. That morning, I woke to the continuous kisses from Hudson on the tip of my nose. It was only then I heard the clanging of dishes muffled through the walls of my bedroom. I rolled over to the clock on my nightstand. It was ten forty-five. Breakfast was already over in the dining room. I should've been serving, but as I brushed the strands of hair from my eyes and looked up at the ceiling, I let out a huge sigh. I needed the sleep. *Thanks, Mom.* I thought to myself. I knew darn well she was the reason Victoria hadn't barged in here yet, shaking me awake the way she used to during our summers off from school when we worked for extra money.

Speaking of money...*maybe we got an order*! I thought to myself. Someone must have put in at least one order in the last twelve hours. I pulled my elbows behind me and propped myself up high enough to pull my computer to my lap. Hudson was now rolled over onto his back. His little feet stretched to the ceiling anxiously waiting for my free hand to rub his belly. I happily obliged and with my other hand, I flipped open the screen and logged into the backend of the website. There was a green circle next to the bell! That notification meant someone put in an order.

"Yes!" I squealed. My voice pierced through me like tires peeling away at a green light. I tapped the button secretly hoping the number was higher than one, but I'd be happy with anything at this point. I glared at the spinning circle as the orders loaded and when they did, I had to do a double-take.

"That can't be right," I said. I refreshed the screen again, but the number was the same. My heart was pounding, hitting heavy like the last round of an MMA fight. I pressed a few more buttons to check the limit I placed last night. It should've been the ten Drake and I agreed on, but when I pulled it up, I noticed right away. I messed up! I added an extra zero. It wasn't a max of ten orders, it was a max of one hundred and sixty had come in overnight! Ten hours and my genius idea was now a successful nightmare.

"Oh no, oh no, what do I do?" My hands were shaking. I leaned over and yanked the drawer of my nightstand open to pull out my phone. Drake's name was at the top of my text list. I tapped his name, fiddled my fingers across the keys to type out a sentence, wondering if he'd be able to read the hysterics I was feeling through a text.

Addie: I messed up! Need to see you now!

I flopped around like a fish in my bed waiting for any sign of Drake to come through my phone, but there was nothing. Not even the dreaded three dots that people had become accustomed to impatiently staring at until words popped up on the screen. It was the last day before Mave's would close for the holidays. Drake was probably too busy in the kitchen cooking to check his phone. I couldn't wait any longer. I threw the sheets off me and swung my body around with so much momentum I almost fell to the floor. Once my feet were underneath me, I ran to the closet.

"Oh my god!" Those were the only three words I was capable of saying at that moment. I was in disbelief. Sixty dozen cookies. Three days. Drake was going to kill me. So was Mave. I shook my head as I yanked a blue sweater off a hanger. I couldn't even think about what Mave was going to think. I threw the sweater over my head, pulled on a pair of jeans, and hobbled into my boots. I swooped up Hudson as I entered the hallway where I met my mother with a plate full of dishes in her hands.

"Good morning sleepyhead," she said.

Her white apron was splattered with remnants of the blueberry pancakes that were on the menu that morning. Her hair was pulled loosely behind her head with a hair tie, but I'd assumed the multiple trips to and from the kitchen were the culprit of the strands that had fallen from its hold. I took a deep breath and forced myself to smile.

"Good morning!" I squeezed out cheerfully, hoping that her mother's instinct wouldn't kick in and see the mess I was behind my smile. Thankfully, she didn't have enough time. Sue was back and the gray bun on top of her head peeked around the corner.

"Becky, can I borrow you for a moment?" Sue asked.

"Sure. Let me put these in the kitchen and I'll be right there." My mother looked over at me. "Where are you off to?"

Thank goodness, for having a dog. "We're going out for our morning walk." My mother smiled. I held in a deep breath knowing I was only half lying. We were going for a walk. Telling her where we were walking to didn't seem to be a necessity. Especially since Drake had shown up the other day at the door looking for me. If I told her I was heading to the coffeehouse, it would only draw up more questions and I didn't have time to give answers.

"Make sure you bundle up. It's cold out there. We got at least six inches last night."

"I will," I said.

My mother gave Hudson a quick tickle behind his floppy ear and then disappeared into the kitchen. When the door swung closed behind her, I let out a huge exhale of pent-up breath and walked swiftly to my jacket that hung in the foyer. My jacket fit snug over my sweater, but I knew I would need the extra layer. With my hat and gloves on and Hudson in tow, I snuck out the front door.

My mother wasn't kidding. The streets of Cold Spring had been painted white for as far as I could see. The snow was still floating down from above me and the freshly shoveled sidewalk that led to the B&B was starting to cover up again. I bent over and let Hudson down onto the sidewalk. He spun around in a few circles before taking a giant leap into the mound of snow beside him. His tiny brown fur disappeared underneath. My heart dropped to my stomach.

"Hudson!" I screamed and slid my feet toward the hole he made fully preparing myself to start digging through with my already cold hands to find him. As I leaned over though, his cute nose popped up and he hopped his way out to my feet. I let out a loud sigh. "Don't scare me like that." I tapped his head and brushed the white flakes from his fur before wrapping my hands around him and tucking him tightly under the arm of my jacket.

It was a quiet morning in town. The snow that had fallen over the once plowed streets were free of tire tracks. Most of the parallel spots along the sidewalks were empty and only a handful of people passed me on my way to the coffeehouse. I peered through the window to see a few families lurking in the booths by the window and a couple seated at the table where I snapped some photos of Drake with his coffee. I bowed my head to look at Hudson who was air swimming in my arms. His little feet were moving so fast hoping that eventually, they'd meet solid ground.

"Hold on little buddy," I said. "Mission is almost complete." I was so close to getting to Drake, but Mave would kill me if I brought a dog into the shop. "Crap!" I hadn't thought of that until now. I was too stunned by seeing six times the number of orders originally planned to think straight. I looked through the window again. Mave was standing behind the register talking to Connie Walton, owner of one of the antique stores in town. I knew Connie well enough to know that Mave wasn't getting out of that conversation anytime soon. Now was my chance. I looked down at Hudson again. "I'm so sorry Hudson." I turned my back to the window and unzipped my jacket enough to wrap it around him. "I'll be quick, I promise."

His little face was staring up at me as I pulled open the door. My hands were clutching tightly to my coat as I walked past the counter and through the door that would lead me behind Mave and into the kitchen.

"Look at you, walking in here like you own the place." Mave stabbed her hand to her hip, but by the smile on her face, I knew she was only playing around. I tried to duck away from her so she wouldn't take notice of Hudson, but right as I stepped behind her, he slid his nose out of my coat. His head was now nestled under my chin and there was no way to hide him.

Mave's hand gripped my arm. "Is that a dog?" Mave whispered. "Adelynne Pine." Her voice was sharp, but still low enough that no one else could hear.

"I know this looks bad, but I promise I have a good excuse," I pleaded. Mave waited.

"One I can't tell you right now, but I have to see Drake. Please." I jutted out my bottom lip.

Mave rolled her eyes and let out a heavy sigh. "Fine," she said. "Make it quick. I don't want customers complaining about dog hair in their food." I nodded, tucked Hudson's head back into my coat, and darted into the kitchen.

Drake was dressed in his usual white chef coat. He was holding tight to a knife, ferociously chopping an onion into bits. Suddenly the magnitude of the gingerbread orders faded as I watched him. I never knew chopping an onion was such a turn on. I could feel the warmth spread from my neck up to my cheeks as I stood there watching him in action. The heat rising in me could very well have been Hudson pressed up against my chest, but since I hadn't been able to stop thinking about the almost kiss between the two of us in

Beacon, I was going to excuse Hudson as being the culprit. The pounding of the knife against the wood block turned into the ticking of the large Main Street clock in Beacon and suddenly I was right back there again outside the glass shop, in Drake's arms with his lips hovering close to mine. Sadly, like that moment, this one didn't last long either. Drake had finished chopping and noticed me standing next to the open door.

"Hey you!" His eyes lit up. He wiped his hands on the towel that hung over his shoulder. "What are you doing here?"

I loved that I was the reason his hazel eyes grew wide, but a lump was forming in my throat, knowing that soon I would have to break the news of what I had done. His brows would fall, his shoulders would sink and the disappointment would overcome him. I hated that I was going to be the reason for it, but I had to tell him. I needed him to help me gather all my thoughts together and figure out what to do.

"Well," I started, "I have some good news and bad news."

"Oh boy. Okay." He dropped himself down onto the edge of the counter and waited. "Give it to me."

I could feel the beads of sweat pooling on my forehead. My cheeks were excruciatingly hot now as I leaned myself against the wall.

"So, remember how we set up the gingerbread orders last night?" I pressed my lips tightly together as Drake nodded. "Well, the good news is we have orders. I checked this morning."

"That's awesome!" Drake slapped his hands together. "What could possibly be bad about that?"

"Well...I may have accidentally messed up the number of orders to max out at. Not may have... I did mess up." Hudson was getting impatient. I leaned my head down toward him and with my forehead against his, I finished. "Instead of ten, I put one hundred and this morning I woke up to sixty orders."

I shut my eyes for a moment and then looked up for Drake's reaction. His mouth was wide open. He wiped his forearm over his furrowed brows, and I could tell he needed a minute to take it in. I watched as he looked down and jiggled his fingers on both of his hands.

"Sixty orders you said?" I watched the crease form between his brows. I nodded and he looked back down, continuing to wiggle his fingers. It seemed like a massive undertaking, but it wasn't until Drake hit me with another number that I fully understood the weight of my mistake.

"Sixty orders...that's about seven hundred cookies."

Seven hundred cookies. What did I do? My lower lip went from pouting into a full-blown shiver. My jaw dropped. Hudson was now clawing his way out of my jacket and my hands were too weak to try and stop him.

"I can't believe I did this." Thank goodness I was already leaning back against the brick wall before Drake said those words out loud. The weight of my body collapsed even harder against it. "I am so sorry. I'll cancel them. I can call them all and tell them there was a huge mix-up and..."

"Now hold on a minute," Drake interrupted my rant. "This may not be as bad as it sounds. The oven can hold six baking sheets at a time. That's over a hundred cookies. I have quite a bit of dough already made in the freezer. Probably enough to make ten dozen or so. If you're up for it, we can pound out the rest tomorrow. That'll leave two days to bake and one day to decorate."

"That seems impossible," I said.

"No, no, we can do it. Sixty order will make us..." Drake paused. He patted his hands on the white of his apron and then pulled out his phone. That's two months of backpay on this place. We have to do it. It's the only way to help save Mave's. You in?"

I squeezed Hudson a little tighter. The lump in my throat made it hard to swallow. I couldn't imagine life in Cold Spring without Mave's Coffeehouse.

Drake seemed confident that with a lot of hard work we could pull this off. I'd never personally baked gingerbread cookies before. Well, that's a lie. I had tried two Christmases ago in my studio in New York City. They were for the office Christmas party. I ended up setting off the smoke alarm and they came out burnt to a crisp. I showed up for work the next day with a fresh batch straight from the corner market. I knew Mave desperately needed our help. So, baking skills or not, there was no other way to answer.

"I'm in," I said.

We shook on it. I looked around at the kitchen where I was going to be spending the next couple of days and the person, I'd be spending it with. The late nights were going to be for a good cause and my company wasn't half bad either.

Hudson had finally had enough. He climbed up out of my coat and started planting endless kisses on my face. Drake and I both laughed, and I took that as my cue to leave.

"I guess I'll see you tomorrow then," I said.

"That you will."

"Okay. See you then."

I shot Drake a half-smile and a wave and nestled Hudson back into my coat long enough to make it back out of the coffeehouse incognito. I set Hudson down on the cold ground and immediately he began to dance around in the snow. I smiled and took in the moment of calm knowing that the next few days were going to be a hectic bake fest.

19

Drake

It felt a little strange heading to the coffeehouse after sunrise. Normally I was in the kitchen prepping while it was still dark outside, but today was the first day of holiday break. Mave's would be quiet and Addie and I would be baking gingerbread nonstop for the next seventy-two hours.

I doubted myself as I turned the key to the back door that would lead me into the kitchen. Sixty dozen gingerbread cookies in three days, that was going to take some serious work and I had no idea what kind of a baker Addie was. Heck, I didn't even know if she was a baker or if this would all fall on me. It would be worth it though if I pulled it off. Addie would be happy, and she'd smile that intoxicating smile. Speaking of Addie, it was only moments after I pulled the bags of chilled dough from the refrigerator that she walked through the door.

"Good morning," I said. Her eyes were half-open. When she pulled her knitted white hat from her head, a tangled mess of waves fell. This was the first time I'd ever seen her undone. I was sure this was how she rolled out of bed in the morning. Her cheeks were smooth and free of added color. Her eyelids weren't as bold as they normally were, but somehow that made the color of her eyes stand out even more. They were almost as dark as the molasses I'd poured to make the gingerbread dough.

"Coffee," she said with a half-smile. "Please tell me I have time to make some coffee."

I laughed as she rubbed her eyes and tried to blink the exhaustion out of them. "You have time. What are you in the mood for?" I asked.

"Something strong. An espresso macchiato sounds fabulous."

"Coming right up!" I said. "The flour is down in that cabinet over there." I pointed to the silver door behind her. "If you want to grab that for me and start sprinkling it on this counter. The rolling pin and cutouts are in the drawer right above. Then, we'll get rolling and cutting."

"Sounds good. Oh, and Drake..." I was almost out of the kitchen when she said my name. I spun around on the butter like floor to face her. "Good morning."

I smiled and gave her a nod before I disappeared to the coffee bar to whip up her macchiato. In the process I decided a shot of espresso might be good for me too and moments later my hands were holding both, returning to the kitchen where Addie was delicately shaking flour from the oversized bag in her hand.

"Here you go," I said. I placed her mug on the counter that was free of any white powder.

"My hero." She gave the bag one final shake before trading it for a long sip of fresh brew. "This tastes like heaven," she said.

"And what exactly does heaven taste like?" I asked.

"Strong and sweet," she laughed. One more slow sip of coffee and Addie was ready. "Okay," she clapped. "Let's do this! Where do we start?"

I threw an apron at her and pulled mine down from the hook near the door. That was always step one. There were days in culinary school when I'd forget my apron and I'd leave at the end of the day looking like a tie-dyed mess and not the pretty hues of bright colors kind of tie-dye. It was more like random splashes of grease and oils.

"I'm going to whip up a few more double batches to get us ahead. Do you think you can handle rolling out the dough and making the gingerbread cutouts?"

A longing look fell across Addie's face. I'm not going to lie, the way her eyes purposely avoided mine made me a little nervous, but after a long pause, she nodded. She tossed her apron around the front of her and tied it tight. With one last tug on her ponytail, she was ready to go.

"Let's do it!" She clapped her hands together and pulled the rolling pin into her hands

"Okay then," I said. "Get to it."

The smell of a good morning at the bakery always started with softened butter. Mix it with a little brown sugar and I was sure if heaven really did taste like something it was the outcome of the two of them as they churned in the mixer while I stood over it. I played with the speeds while I watched Addie pull the dough from the wrapped plastic and place it on the flour-covered counter. She picked up the rolling pin and using all her weight she leaned it into the dough.

I pierced my lips together and tried not to laugh at how the dough hugged tightly to the roller when she lifted it. The stone look on her face showed off her determination and my eyes fixated on how adorable her creased forehead was as she attempted to roll the dough out again.

"What the heck," I heard her murmur under her breath.

It was almost time for me to pour the molasses into the mixing bowl, but I wasn't sure I could let Addie torture herself any longer.

"Need some help?" I asked.

She answered with a hard no. "I can do it." A hefty puff escaped from her mouth to remove a strand of hair that had fallen in front of her eye.

I lifted up the measuring cup full of molasses and slowly poured it in. I glanced over again. Addie chucked the rolling pin off the other side of the counter. The force against the metal cabinets echoed and Addie's eyes flinched. She looked over at me, her brows lifted. She shrugged her shoulders and I counted. There were maybe four seconds of silence before I couldn't hold it in any longer. I laughed and thankfully she joined in. She threw her hands up.

"Okay," she said, "I admit, baking isn't my forte. My mother's the one who rolls out all the dough for the sugar cookies. I usually pick put the shapes, press them into the already flat dough and don't think about it again until it's time to decorate. Help me. Please."

The same pouty lip look that had gotten me into this gingerbread scheme was working its magic once again. Her bottom lip protruded out and the corner of her eyes dropped in my direction.

"All right," I said. I rinsed off my hands and patted them on the towel draped over my shoulder. "You have to coat the roller with some flour. It helps to keep the dough from sticking. I pulled another rolling pin from the drawer." The smell of molasses that overpowered me at the mixing bowl was replaced with a subtle floral scent. It grew as I moved closer to stand next to Addie. "Take this," I handed her a small measuring cup. "Grab some flour from the bag and sprinkle it on. Not too much though. You don't want to dry out the dough."

Addie pulled the bag of flour between us and reached inside. "It's all stuck together."

"That's all right. Sift it around a little to break it up." I should've been clearer. When I said to sift, I meant carefully. You have to do that with flour. If not, it goes everywhere. I thought about the word... carefully, and opened my mouth to say it just in case, but it was too late. Addie swept the measuring cup up from the bottom of the bag and as my mouth opened to speak, I was met with a huge dusting of dry white powder. I felt it fall against my face and pieces of it fluttered in my eye each time I blinked. I inhaled in surprise. That was a mistake.

"Oh my gosh," Addie called out. I was coughing. Or maybe gagging, trying to clear the flour from my throat. Addie's hands fell heavy on my back. First, it was only once, then it came again. The thump was harder than before and quickly the timing between each of them was less and less. "Are you okay? I'm so sorry."

With my hand to my mouth, I made my way to the fridge and twisted open a bottle of water. I chugged it down and took gasping breaths in between each gulp. When it was gone, my breathing was heavy, but the nutty flavor in my mouth was gone.

"Well, that was fun." I fell against the fridge and stared in her direction.

Her hands covered her mouth and all I could see was the flutter of her lashes. I couldn't tell whether or not she wanted to laugh or cry. Her hands slid down her face and suddenly her lips parted to let out a high-pitched laugh. I crossed my arms and glared at her trying to force the muscles in my face not to take part.

"I really am sorry," she said in between her bouts of laughter.

"I can tell." The sarcasm escaped me, but the tiny smirk that followed eased her mind. She wiped her hands over her apron and waved me over.

"Come here," she said.

She pulled the towel from my shoulder when I was close enough and gripped her fingers around it. I wondered if she could hear the heavy rhythm of my heartbeat as she reached up and swiped the softness of the towel across my face. Her dark eyes were looking right into mine and for a moment I stood still and let her clear the flour from my forehead. Then with one hand, I reached up and gently folded my hand around her forearm. Her hand fell to my shoulder. My other hand slowly reached around her back.

"Do you forgive me?" Her eyes longed for an answer.

"Almost," I said. I moved my hand slowly behind her so she wouldn't notice. Then I patted my hand in a mound of flour that lay on the counter and in one swift movement, I ever so gently swiped my fingers across her face. The remnants of my handprint were now spread, in white powder, across her cheek. Her mouth dropped open.

"You did not!" Her voice rose along with her smile.

"Now, I forgive you," I said.

"And here I was, trying to be nice and help clean up the mess I made. Oh, wait... looks like I missed a spot. Hold on. Right....here!" A wave a white smoke once again fell against my cheeks and the two of us leaped into an all-out flour war. Clouds of white blinded me. I tossed whatever I could grab in her direction and hoped I hit my target. I took my gloved hand and scooped a mound from the open bag on the counter.

"Don't you dare!" The sound of her voice was as playful as the look in her wide eyes. The crease on her forehead deepened the closer I stepped.

"Put the measuring cup down slowly and I'll surrender," I said.

"Promise?" Addie asked. I nodded.

The sound of surrender came when the measuring cup hit the counter. I kept my word and dumped the pile in my hand into the garbage. The two of us laughed in unison. Our breaths were heavy as we examined the aftermath. There was flour at our feet, on our aprons, and at least a dusting on every countertop.

"I think there's plenty of flour on the rolling pin now," I said.

"Oh, you're funny," Addie said as she flung the towel back over my shoulder. When it landed, she was still standing only inches from me. Our eyes locked again, and I could feel her hand clench as it rested on my shoulder. We stood this close outside the glass shop in Beacon and I almost gave in then. If it wasn't for that car, I probably would have. But now, there was nothing to distract us. Only the two of us were inside that coffeehouse. The nerves inside me grew and before I could push them back down, I leaned my lips down to meet hers. I slid my hands around her waist to pull her closer. The warmth from her lips folded around mine a few more times before she gently pulled away. I let my eyes stay closed a little longer because I didn't want that moment to end, but it had to.

"Wow." Those were the next words out of Addie's mouth. She whispered them while I struggled to open my eyes.

"Yeah," I laughed. Addie pulled her hands from my chest and turned away from me. The oven bell rang, and I took that as our sign.

"Back to work?" Addie turned toward the ball of dough and grabbed the rolling pin.

"Back to work," I said. "Let me know if you need any help."

She agreed and the two of us went back to baking as if nothing happened.

20

Addie

Drake kissed me. Drake *kissed* me. That phrase floated through my mind for most of the night and was the reason I was now standing here adjacent to the Hudson River as the sun rose from behind me. I was tired of tossing and turning and reliving the moment over in my mind. When the first bit of light peaked through my window, I gave in. I threw the covers off me and headed to the one place I knew would help me clear my head.

Even Hudson wasn't fully awake when I clipped his collar over his fur that morning. It wasn't until we were halfway to the river that he found his energy. He stood in front of me now, bounding from one side of me to the other playing tug-of-war with his leash. Darkness was still covering most of the sky as I tried to capture the magic of a quiet morning in Cold Spring. Hudson's sudden movements didn't make for the best photos. Each time he would tug, the hand holding the leash would shake. I tried to wait until he surrendered each time to snap a photo. I'd adjust the lens and the shutter speed as the lighting changed to try and find the right exposure for each photo.

That's one of the things that Brody had tried to teach me before I left the city. I tried to turn up the shutter speed to grasp the velocity of the crashing waves against the rocks. Brody told me a higher shutter speed helped to catch fast-moving objects. Aperture was a word I still couldn't pronounce correctly, but I was getting the hang of what it did when it came to photos. I knew that if I focused mostly on the rocks the waves were bouncing off, the scenery that fell to the background would blur. That was my intention.

"Hudson, sit," I said after looking at my last dozen photos. They were all blurry and not the parts I was aiming for. Hudson's teeth were gripped around his leash and I couldn't help but laugh as he snarled. "Hudson, let go. Let go, Hudson. Hudson, sit." My eight weeks of puppy classes were failing me. I tried to shake the leash in hopes Hudson would release it, but every time I did, he pulled harder. I continued to shout commands and he continued to ignore them. If I had known I had an audience, I probably wouldn't have been so persistent.

"He really loves that rope." I shot my head around and tried to squint through the rising sun to see where the voice was coming from. There was movement over by the gazebo. It didn't take long for the silhouette to come into view. It was a rarity I saw Drake outside of his chef coat but considering the bite of cold coming off the river that morning, I understood the heavy coat and gray beanie. I didn't so much like that I couldn't see the gelled curls that usually lay flat against his head.

"You're up early," he said. His body was now hiding the sun and I was able to fully open my eyes again.

I could tell he was trying to make this encounter less awkward.

I played along, but even I knew we were going to have to talk about that kiss eventually.

"Yeah, I thought I'd take advantage of the isolation. You know, before the crowds roll in."

"I can leave you alone if you want." He shoved his hands deeper into his pockets.

I did want to take more photos, but I had to admit, I liked the fact that even after spending twelve hours with him the day before, I still wasn't tired of seeing those green eyes staring back at me.

"No, no, you don't have to," I said. "I don't think I'll be too productive anyway with this guy."

Drake's tall stature melted as he bent down to Hudson's level. "Come here, boy." He patted his knees. Hudson's ears perked up and he struggled to get his fast-moving legs off the iced blacktop. I laughed as all four of his furry paws fell behind him and he somersaulted into Drake's arms. "He's a cutie."

"He sure is," I said. "He loves it up here. It's his first time out of the city and I think he'll have a hard time going back."

"Why do you say that?" Drake pressed his nose up against Hudson's face and soon Hudson's tiny pink tongue was giving Drake all the kisses he would allow.

"For starters, he loves all the attention he's been getting. He rolls in the snow every chance he gets and there's a little less noise up here. It's usually hard for me to take him outside because he jumps every time he hears a horn, and well, if you know New York City..."

"It never sleeps."

I nodded as Drake finished the sentence for me. "Pretty much."

"Do you think you'd ever come back home?" Drake asked.

"Oh gosh." I slid my feet to the nearest bench and lowered myself onto it. I let out a heavy sigh and watched my breath escape into the air. I'd asked myself that same question so many times. "I think about it sometimes. Don't get me wrong, I love New York and I love that every day I discover something new around a new corner I've never been before. Then I come back here and...it's like I'm a whole different person."

"Small towns will do that to you," Drake said. He was still cuddling with Hudson. His black boots took a few steps closer.

"Yeah. There's something about being able to see the stars at night and the way people wave to you as you walk by that makes you..." Drake too was now sitting on the bench beside me.

"Happy..." he said. I kind of liked the way he was finishing my sentences. I looked over at him and nodded. "I get it."

I shivered at the gust of wind that rolled off the river and tangled my hair in front of my face. I lifted my gloved hand up to sweep it away, but Drake beat me to it. I felt the coldness of leather brush against my temple as Drake swept my hair behind my ear. We were staring at each other the same way we were right before he kissed me in the kitchen. I held my breath, desperately hoping he had the courage to it again. It shocked me the first time and I had to admit, I didn't handle it with much grace. I barely talked to him for the rest of the day.

We spent all day yesterday in our respective corners. I cut out the gingerbread and swapped trays in and out of the oven. Drake mixed as much dough as he possibly could and when ten o'clock came around, the two of us could barely keep our eyes open.

When we said goodnight, that was the only time we spoke more than two words to each other until now.

This time... don't pull away. I thought, waiting for him to lean closer, but he didn't.

"We should probably get you home. It's freezing down here. I don't want you to catch pneumonia. We still have cookies to make and a whole lot to decorate."

"Right," I flinched. By that point, Hudson was getting impatient. He jumped out of Drake's arms into my lap. I looked down at him and he whimpered.

"Looks like he's ready for a little warmth too," Drake said.

"I think so." I cleared my throat and swallowed all the hope that Drake would kiss me away.

"I'll see you in a bit then?"

I pushed myself off the bench and wrapped my arms around Hudson. "Absolutely! Make sure the coffee's ready." I winked.

"You got it," Drake said. With one last smile, I turned away from him and made the trek back home.

In a couple of hours, Drake and I would be back to business and as much as I liked being able to steal glances of him sifting flour and mixing dough, I was starting to enjoy the moments outside of the kitchen more. It wasn't only Cold Spring that turned me into a different person. Drake did too. I let my guard down with him. I never talked about my dad to anyone, but I loved sharing old memories with Drake. In the years since my dad has been gone, I couldn't remember a time where I'd laughed as hard as I did during that flour fight.

Coming home this year wasn't only about Dylan. I realized that now. It was about figuring out who I was again and what I really wanted and the one thing I knew for sure over the past week was that I liked the way I was when Drake was around. I wasn't sure that in a week's time I was going to be ready to let that person go.

21

Addie

The B&B smelled of fresh maple and blueberries when it was time for me to head to the coffeehouse. Hudson was chewing his bone on the couch in the sunroom. I gave him a quick pat on his belly before pulling a thick, black fleece over me. Breakfast in the main room was about over when I opened the door that separated my quaint living quarters from the family business.

"Good morning sweetheart." My mother smiled at me with a stack of dirty dishes in her hand. "I saved you a plate of pancakes. They're in the oven so they'd keep warm."

"Thanks, Mom, but I've got to run."

"Not before you eat," she said. Her eyes widened and I knew that meant she wasn't taking no for an answer. I pulled out my phone and typed a quick text to Drake.

Running a little late. Be there as soon as I can. Sorry!

I followed behind my mother, yanked a fork from the drawer beside the stove, and pulled the warm plate from the oven. I sliced the stack of pancakes into tiny triangles and turned to face the wall of white subway tiles so that I could shove a few bites into my mouth. I should've known better than to think my mother wouldn't notice.

"Adelynne Dawn!" She yelled from behind me. "What is going on with you?"

I mumbled out *nothing* through a mouthful of pancakes, but I don't think it actually sounded coherent. Without another word, my mother led me and my blueberry stained teeth out into the now empty dining room. She pulled out a cross back chair and motioned for me to sit.

"Something is going on young lady." Her voice was stern. Her brows furrowed and her lips puckered in worry. "You are not leaving this house until you tell me what it is."

I was still chewing the last forkful of pancakes, so there was a bit of silence before I confessed. "Okay, but I need you to promise me you won't tell anyone." I held out my pinkie.

"Pinkie swear," she said wrapping her pinkie around mine.

"Drake told me that Mave's Coffeehouse is in trouble. They're behind on rent and if they didn't find a way to bring in more revenue soon, Mave's would have to close its doors for good."

"Oh, poor Mave." The radiant glow escaped my mother's cheeks and a glazed expression filled her eyes. "That coffeehouse is her whole life."

"I know," I said. "That's why I'm trying to help her. Drake and I, we launched a website to test out online ordering and I had this great idea to do gingerbread cookie orders. You know, for a last-minute holiday party idea. I thought that it would help test out the online ordering as well as bring in a little extra revenue. If it went well, it could be something Mave could incorporate at every holiday."

I looked up at my mom. The longing gaze in her eyes was followed by a smile. She placed her hands on mine. "Oh Addie, that's a wonderful idea."

"It would've been, but I messed up. I accidentally set the website to allow for one-hundred orders instead of ten, and well, the idea was so popular that it brought in sixty orders. That's sixty dozen cookies Mom! Drake didn't want to cancel them because it would've been bad for business, so we decided to go for it. Yesterday, we spent more than twelve hours making dough and we were able to bake about twenty dozen. Today we have to make the rest and tomorrow we have to decorate and package them all to be ready for pick-up on the twenty-third. It's a mess, but Drake is sure we can pull it off."

"Oh honey," she said. She squeezed my hands. "Look at you trying to save the world. You certainly are your father's daughter."

I pulled my hands from hers and pushed myself off the chair before she could see the wetness build in my eyes. I messed up, big time and now Drake was working on his days off and we were scrambling to try to put this all together all without Mave knowing. I hated that we were keeping this from her, but I didn't want to stress her out even more than she probably already was.

"I don't know," I said. "What if we can't do it?"

"You will." She took my face in her hands and her eyes widened as she blinked back tears. "Have faith sweet girl."

"Thank you." I fell into her arms and a part of me hoped that the strength she exuded this past couple of years since my dad had been gone would somehow transfer into me.

"Now, finish up your pancakes and go get to work!" I laughed and squeezed her a little tighter before letting go.

She swept her fingers through my hair and kissed my forehead before she left me alone to shove the rest of my breakfast down my throat. I was still a bit frazzled at the number of cookies we had to make today, but the weight I'd felt on my chest seemed to lighten after talking with my mother.

I grabbed my purse from the hook by the door and tugged my hat over my ears. It was another snowy day in Cold Spring, but I embraced the scenery as I watched the featherlike flakes dance askew across the clear blue sky. It was the kind of snow that was built for snowmen. They didn't disappear when they hit the ground, they piled up on top of each other leaving the perfect place for the sun to glisten. *I wish I had time to build a snowman today.* I thought as I crossed Main Street, but I knew I didn't. I had a coffeehouse to save and that came before any charcoal pipe.

I pulled the door to Mave's open and smiled as I took in the nutty smell that filled the coffeehouse. Drake was standing behind the counter with a cup in hand.

"You ready?" He handed me a warm cup.

"I will be after a sip of this."

I took the cup back into the kitchen and Drake followed. The talk I had with my mother this morning almost dug up enough courage for me to address yesterday's kiss, but when he looked over at me taking that first sip of coffee, I knew it wasn't going to happen. I watched the corners of his lips curl up for a second before he pulled his eyes away from me and back at the mixer full of butter and molasses.

Down at the river, Drake had a chance to kiss me again, and yet he didn't. I was afraid that if I brought it up, if the two of us started to talk about it, that he would tell me it was a mistake. He would say that he got caught up in the moment. The last thing I wanted that kiss to be was a mistake and truthfully, even if it wasn't, Drake lived here in Cold Spring, and in less than a week I'd be headed back to the city. Whatever this was would end as fast as it started, and I wasn't ready for it to be over yet. So, I said nothing. I wanted to hold that moment close for as long as I could before reality stole it away.

22

Drake

Even in between the high speed of the mixer I could hear her laughing. I'd look over my shoulder when she did and see Addie stare at her phone. She'd tuck it away and get back to rolling out another ball of gingerbread dough. Christmas music was playing in the background and I'd smile while she hummed along.

The dough was no longer sticking to the rolling pin. After cutting out close to four hundred cookies, Addie was starting to get the hang of this baking thing. Heck, by now I think Mave would even feel confident enough to hire her on. If she lived here that is, but she didn't. I tried not to think about that as I watched her pick up the cookie cutter and press it into the flattened dough.

Another *ding* came from the back pocket of Addie's jeans. She pulled off her gloves and slid it out to take a look. This time she tapped her fingers across the screen, but she didn't laugh. The look on her face was vacant.

"How's it going over there?" I asked.

"Pretty good! After this batch goes in the oven, we only have twenty-four dozen more to go."

"Everything okay?" I asked.

"Oh yeah. Victoria keeps sending me pictures of her and Dylan. They're building a snowman outside the B&B. Well, she and her husband are building the snowman. Dylan's not too sure what's going on. How cute is this?"

Addie turned her phone toward me so I could see Dylan in his blue snowsuit and brown hat with a monkey face on the front. Victoria was holding him in one hand and a carrot in the other. His toothless smile was wide.

"He's a cutie," I said.

"He sure is." Addie looked back down at her phone and I hated the way her brown eyes grimaced at the photo. I could tell she wanted to be there too. Staring at gingerbread cookies for hours on end was only fun for so long, even for me. "Why don't you take a break. Go have some fun with them," I said.

She looked up at me and I loved the way the smooth caramel in her eyes lit up. "What? No. That's okay. We have a lot of work to do here."

"And we'll do it," I said, "but not if we get burnt out. Really, go."

"Are you sure?" Addie asked.

"Positive."

Her eyes widened and her lips parted to let out a low-toned shriek. "Thank you! I won't be gone for long. Thirty minutes tops."

She untied her apron and threw it on the counter and gave her hands a quick wash before turning off the oven. Her fleece was hanging by the door. She almost forgot it with how fast she ran out. I reveled in the spectacle. Adelynne Pine intrigued me. Every move. When she popped her head back in to grab her fleece, she took a long look at me.

"Why don't you come too?"

"Oh no, that's okay," I said.

"Come on. You said it yourself. We won't get anything done if we get burnt out. Please." Her eyes pleaded with me.

"All right. I'll come." She clapped her hands together and smiled. She thought she had to twist my arm, but honestly, I was secretly hoping that she would ask. It would be nice to see Addie be able to relax while she was here. She was supposed to be on vacation, but her delicate heart and love for this town had her sweating in a windowless kitchen with me for hours on end. She deserved this. Maybe with both did.

I knew I was right when the two of us walked through the thick snow in front of the B&B. Victoria waved frantically. She handed Dylan over to the tall man standing next to her. I'd assumed he was Victoria's husband. She talked about him often, but I'd never met him.

"Hey you guys! Did you come to build some snowmen?" Victoria asked.

"We sure did!" Addie yelled back.

"Oh, thank goodness!" Victoria pulled the pink hat from her head. Her blonde hair fell matted down to her shoulders. "We made the mom and the dad. You two can make the kids. One boy and one girl. I'm going to make some hot chocolate." She looked back toward the snowmen. "Trent, let's go inside."

The tall man now had a name. Trent nodded and lifted his knees high with each step he took towards us. The snow was thick. It must've fallen heavy during the hours Addie and I were stuck inside.

"Trent, this is Drake." Victoria introduced us. "He's the new baker down at Mave's."

"Catering manager," Addie said. She turned to me with a wink.

"Sorry, catering manager..." Victoria repeated.

"Oh right. I've heard a lot about you," Trent said. He reached out the hand that wasn't wrapped tightly around Dylan.

"Same here. Nice to meet you," I said.

"I'm putting Drake and Addie to work. They're going to finish our little snowmen family. Have fun you two."

Victoria and Trent waved as they trekked through the snow back into the B&B, leaving Addie and me out in the cold alone.

"Well, it looks like we're about to make some snow kids," Addie laughed.

"If your snowman building skills are anything like your baking skills, I think we're in trouble," I said.

I couldn't help but smirk at the sigh that slipped from Addie's lips. She was not glaring at me with her arms crossed.

"I may not know how to roll dough, but you don't grow up in Cold Spring and not know how to build a snowman." She reached out too fast for me to take cover and before I knew it, she was throwing a big lump of snow into my chest. The denseness hit me heavily, but Addie found my pain amusing.

"Ow!" I yelled.

"That's what you get for making fun of me."

"Noted," I winced. "Let's see it then."

I reached down and started piling up the snow to make the bottom half of my snowman. Addie stood a few feet away doing the same. I let her concentrate on the first snowball before I brought up the heavy stuff. Once she was on the second ball where the buttons would go, I wiped my hands of the snowflakes that were stuck to my gloves and turned to her.

"Hey," I said, "about the other day..."

She looked at me, her brows furrowed. "What about it?"

"I just wanted to be sure that we were okay. You know... the kiss."

"Oh." Addie's hands froze on top of the mound of snow. She looked over at me with even rosier cheeks than she had when we started. "Yeah, of course. Why wouldn't we be?"

"You haven't said much since it happened." My calves were burning. I fell onto my knees and immediately regretted it once the snow seeped through my jeans, but I tried to ignore the temperature drop of my body heat.

"I guess maybe I was afraid," she said. I envied her. Instead of falling into the snow, she pushed herself up to stand.

"Afraid of what?" I asked.

"Afraid of what it meant." She lowered her head to look down at her fidgeting hands. "Afraid of how I felt. That it was an impulse. That you'd regret it."

That kiss made me feel a lot of things. Regret was not one of them and I hated to hear that was even a thought in her mind. My knees were numb. I couldn't feel them as I pushed myself out of the snow. It hurt to walk towards her, but it was worth every step. I pulled her hands in mine.

"Addie, I haven't regretted a single moment I've spent with you since we met."

"Not even the fact that I got you into this whole gingerbread cookie mess?"

I laughed. If it had been anyone else, my answer might have been different, but Addie's idea had the best of intentions and if we could pull it off, it would mean there was a chance we could save Mave's. Without the gingerbread cookie idea, we wouldn't be standing here talking about a kiss because I'm sure there wouldn't have even been one and that would've been the biggest regret of all.

"Not even the gingerbread cookie mess," I said. She finally looked up at me. "I didn't kiss you on impulse. I kissed you because it's something I've wanted to do for a while and when I saw a chance...I took it. I'd probably do it again too. Maybe even right now if your sister wasn't creepily staring at us through that bay window."

"What?" Addie's voice raised. She shot her head around and Victoria's eyes shot open wide when she realized that we caught her. She backed away from the windows and flung the curtains closed. "She is relentless."

"Ha, I like her," I said. "She's gutsy."

"Yeah. She's something." Addie rolled her eyes and looked back up into mine.

"I like you, Addie," I said. I still had no feeling in my knees, but it was the opposite for my heart. Saying those words to her made it beat so hard. I thought it might crack its way out of my chest. "I like spending time with you. There's been this gray cloud over my head knowing that my parents are coming. I dread all the things I know my dad will say, but since you came around, I haven't thought about it for a second. You've made me happy and I get it, you know, I'm going to wake up one day next week and you'll be gone. I guess I didn't want you to leave without knowing what it was like to kiss you."

"Oh yeah?" I felt Addie's leg brush up against mine as she stepped closer. "Tell me, what is it like?"

I lowered my lips closer until they were hovering only inches from hers. "It's like that moment, after spending the day outside in newly fallen snow," I whispered. "Your whole body is shaking, and you sit down next to a roaring fire. The heat hits you just right and suddenly the warmth surges through you. You take a deep breath and..."

I wasn't able to finish the sentence before Addie pulled my lips against hers. The wetness of her gloves were cold against my neck, but the way she folded her lips around mine instantly thawed every part of me. I held her in that embrace until I heard the front door slam. When I opened my eyes, I saw Victoria standing on the front porch with a wide grin.

"The hot chocolate is ready," she yelled. Her hands were folded across her chest.

"Thanks, Victoria." Both Addie and I responded and when she walked back inside the two of us looked at each other and smiled. Addie looped her arm through mine and the two of us walked together up the front porch away fragments of a snowmen family that we never did finish.

23

Addie

The break of snowmen building and hot chocolate by the Christmas tree was exactly what Drake and I needed to resurge our energy. We ended up finishing all sixty dozen cookies after that. We even made a few more in case of mistakes.

We were now standing in the kitchen the following morning staring at the sea of endless gingerbread cookies. All sixty dozen were now separated into shapes. The grand plan was to decorate every single one by the afternoon. They'd have enough time to cool and we'd come back to package them up in the evening. We'd grab two snowflakes, two hearts, two stars, two ornaments, and four gingerbread men, all in that order, and tuck them neatly into the cellophane bags I picked up from the craft store over in Newburgh. It was going to be a lot of work, but we were so close.

"Do you want to start with the snowflakes or the gingerbread men?" Drake asked. For some reason, he looked even more handsome today than he usually did. He was leaning against the counter in a blue t-shirt and faded jeans. His hair screamed bed head and his bloodshot eyes exposed last night's phone conversation between the two of us. The one that ended around two in the morning.

"Unless you want your gingerbread men to look like Frankenstein, I think I better start with the snowflakes."

I had years of practice spreading colored frosting across a sugar cookie and dousing it with sprinkles, but when it came to being meticulous, well... my mother can vouch for me on that one. I wasn't neat and I wasn't detailed. After our "Cookies with Santa" night was over, she'd wipe up the tablecloths. When she would come to my spot she'd say, *you can always tell where Addie was sitting.* I guess even five-year-olds were able to keep sprinkles on their plate better than I was. A sea of red and green was always scattered in heaping mountains where I was.

"Haha! That's true," Drake laughed. "Here..." He pushed himself from the counter and reached into the pocket of his jeans. "I printed these out for you. That way you don't have to think of a design. Follow these photos."

"Thanks!" I wasn't even offended that Drake had no faith in my cookie decorating skills. I was more impressed he knew me well enough to bring photos of cookie designs for me to follow. I smiled at him, hoping that was enough to hide the pit in my stomach that I now felt every time I looked at him. Of course, I would fall for a guy in my hometown... once I left.

"Here's your piping bag." Drake slid a triangular looking piece of plastic toward me. "You'll want to fill it with icing to about here." I took a marker and put a dot where his finger pointed. He already had one piping bag filled. He held it tightly in one hand and guided the bag with the other. "Then, you'll squeeze gently like this and when you're done, you flick your wrist and give the bag a quick pull. Tada!"

I took in a deep breath. If mine could look half as good as Drake's first attempt, we'd be golden. I watched him decorate a couple more. It came so easy for him. The stone look on his face as he traced little zig-zags across the arms of the gingerbread men made me chuckle. Everything I didn't know I needed was standing next to me. I fought the urge to lean in and kiss him again the way I did outside in the snow in front of the B&B. Standing so close to him made it hard.

"Okay," I clapped, breaking up the thoughts in my head. "Here I go!" I stepped over to my side of the table and after filling the piping bag, I began to decorate.

*

Five hours later we barely had two-hundred cookies decorated. My fingers were permanently stuck in the shape of a piping bag. When I tried to unfold them, they fell right back into position. We were running out of time.

"I need to take a break," I said. I pulled off my apron and threw my gloves in the trash. "I've got to run and take out Hudson, maybe press my fingers underneath a book to straighten them back out again. You should eat some lunch," I said.

"Yeah, maybe you're right. I'll head over to Salvatore's and pick up a pizza. What do you like?" I felt my face scrunch and immediately Drake took notice. "What? You don't like pizza?"

"No, I love pizza. Salvatore's over Gus's though?"

"Ah, I see where this is going," Drake laughed. "Salvatore's is closer, and they put extra parmesan on my pizza without me having to ask."

"Ugh," I said. "Fine. Pepperoni works for me."

"Pepperoni it is. I'll see you in a bit."

I waved and ran out the door. The tears started flowing down my cheeks as soon as the cold air hit my face. They froze like icicles above my lips. There was no way we were going to finish all these cookies in time. I failed Mave. I failed this town and worst of all, I failed Drake. I was the one who dragged him into this. Not only would Mave's still be in jeopardy of going under, but Mave would be furious when she finds out. She would find out. We'd have to tell her. *How could I let this happen?* I thought. Anger poured out of my eyes and the mix of salt and mascara burned. I didn't even try to hide it when I walked inside the B&B where Sue and my mother were standing at the front desk.

"Sweetheart," my mother said. She reached her arms out for me. "What is the matter?"

"I don't think we can do it. We're so close, but we're running out of time."

"Okay, now." She pulled my head into her chest and wrapped her arms tightly around me. "How can I help?"

I stopped crying long enough to catch my breath. "Do you have five extra pairs of hands I could borrow?" I laughed, but if it was possible, I would've taken them.

"I don't have five pairs, but I have one."

"Thanks, Mom, but you have enough work to do around here. I couldn't ask you to..."

"You're not asking. I'm offering," she said. "I can get everything set up for dinner tonight, head over for a couple of hours, and still be back before the guests are seated in the dining area."

I hadn't been home in two years. I abandoned my mother when she needed me the most. I didn't know how to handle the loss of my father and I turned my back on my family, yet here she is, after all that, coming through in a moment I needed her. She was the most selfless person I'd ever known.

"You don't know how much this means to me and Mave. Thank you, thank you, thank you." I threw my arms around her. "I'm going to take Hudson for a quick walk and then head back. Come whenever you can."

Hudson must've heard my voice. He was waiting in the hallway when I opened the door and came galloping toward me. "Hey bud!" I swept him into my arms and nudged my head into his tangled fur. It felt so good to be home. At that moment, with Hudson in my arms, I felt completely content. For the last few years, I'd been working nonstop in the city. I'd constantly been knocked off the ladder I was trying to climb. I was getting nowhere, yet in the week I'd been back in Cold Spring, it was as if all the pieces had fallen into place. Maybe I'd left to find something that was already here to begin with.

24

Drake

The scent of cinnamon and nutmeg had surrounded me for days. Grease and oregano were a welcome change when I lifted the top of the pizza box. My stomach was growling so loud by the time I pulled the first slice. The melted mozzarella stretched across my plate as I inhaled the first bite. I'd been known to eat an entire pizza in one sitting on more than one occasion. If Addie didn't hurry, all she'd be left with would be crumbs.

I needed all the energy I could get at this point. The amount of work to pull off sixty dozen cookies may have been slightly underestimated when I did the math. We weren't even halfway through decorating and still had to package all of them to be ready first thing in the morning. It seemed impossible, but I had already decided if I had to pull an all-nighter, I would. Mave took a chance on me when she gave me this job. I owed her that much and Addie was in this mess because I confided in her.

There were still three slices left in the pizza box when I saw Addie coming up the street. She looked more relaxed than when she left. Her feet were moving swiftly along the sidewalk and her eyes radiated joy. I guess a walk and fresh air was what she needed. Addie yanked the door open and lunged inside.

"I have good news!" she screeched. "My mom is coming to help decorate. She should be here soon."

"That is good news," I said. I tried to remain calm and collected, but inside I was jumping for joy. Another set of hands would really help move things along. "I saved you some pizza."

"Yes, my hero." Addie sunk into the chair next to me and swiped a slice from the box. "Gosh, this is so good. I don't care what anyone says about the ginormous slices of pieces you get on the streets of New York. None of those compare to this hometown pizza. Even if it is Salvatore's"

"It seems your list of reasons not to go back to New York is growing," I joked. Addie looked over at me wide-eyed. I winked at her and spun around to the back of the coffeehouse. "I'm going to get back to decorating. See you in a few."

I figured I'd let my last comment sink in. I knew it was selfish, but the way Addie talked about New York City, it didn't seem like she felt as if she belonged there. She was doing more photography and creative work here in the last week than her work allowed her to do since she started. I was grasping for anything that made me think she'd stay longer than Christmas and while I was squeezing the frosting onto the cookies, I couldn't help but think of what life would be like if she did.

I didn't get a whole lot of time to think of future plans. I got as far as New Year's Eve before voices from the other room snapped me back to reality. Addie's mom must have arrived. I heard Addie's voice yell, "I can't believe this!" Then she came running into the kitchen. "Drake!"

"What's up?" I set the pastry bag down on the counter. Addie pointed at the opening that lead out into the front of the coffeehouse. I looked over to see Addie's mother walking through, but she wasn't alone. She was followed by Victoria, the woman who worked at the front desk of the B&B and... Mave. My fists clenched. Mave knew. I tried to catch Addie's stare, but she was so excited to have them all there that she didn't look my way.

"I brought reinforcements," Addie's mother said. "I figured you could use all the help you could get."

"We sure can!" Addie said. "Grab an apron. Drake can show you what to do. He's the expert."

Mave walked slowly past the oven to show everyone where the aprons were kept. She pulled one out for herself and draped it around her neck. I followed her every move. She took the long way around the island toward me. She picked up the piping bag sitting on the counter between the two of us and started decorating.

"Did you think I wouldn't find out about this?" Mave whispered. I knew when Mave was angry and this wasn't it. There was a gentleness in her voice.

"No, I knew you would. Nothing ever gets by you," I admitted.

"Then why didn't you tell me?"

"You saved me when you gave me this job. I wanted to do the same for you."

Mave bowed her head closer to the counter to try and hide it, but I saw the corners of her lips raise. I swung my arm around her and pulled her in close. It was a rare moment for Mave to show emotion, but I embraced it before she slapped her hand onto my stomach.

"Get to work you," she laughed.

"All right, all right. Time for a baking lesson," I shouted and waved everyone around the table.

I couldn't help but look around that room and smile. Without even knowing it, I built a family in this town. Here was a group of people willing to toss their to-do's out the window to spend hours in this kitchen, decorating cookies to save a landmark. With four extra pairs of hands, we were able to finish decorating the cookies in record time, and by the time the sun went down most of them were already packaged. There were only two or three dozen that we decided to leave until the morning.

Addie volunteered to come in early and finish up since she'd be there to hand them all out to everyone who was picking up their orders. I offered to help, but with my parents coming in tomorrow, Addie politely declined. It was only her and I in the kitchen when it was time to close the shop.

"Are you sure?" I asked flicking the light switch. The room went dark.

"Definitely. Spend time with your parents. I've got this."

"Okay, but if you need anything, call me."

"I will."

I pushed open the door that led out to Main Street. The snow was still coming down and the sidewalks were covered in a thick blanket of white. Fresh tire marks lay in the road where the snowplow had come through.

"You'll bring them to Christmas Eve right?" Addie asked. I had almost forgotten about Christmas Eve at the B&B.

"You know, why not. It might help ease the tension to have others around and who can pass up cookies and milk?"

We both laughed standing under the glare of the streetlight. Addie shifted back and forth and I stood like a deer in headlights with my hands tucked into my pockets. It was crazy to think I was about to go a whole day without seeing her.

"Good luck tomorrow," she said.

"Yeah. You too. Let me know how it goes." She nodded. "Goodnight Addie."

I wanted to kiss her, but this was a small town and I wasn't sure if she was ready for that gossip. Instead, I stood still and let her lead.

"Goodnight Drake." She placed her hand on my shoulder and pulled herself up onto her tiptoes to press her cold lips against my cheek. I smiled. That was enough for me. When she fell back onto her heels I looked down into her eyes. I could see glistening of the street lights shine back at me. I brushed my bare hand across her cheek and winked at her before she backed away. I stood next to that lamppost and watched her cross the street. A mix of emotions washed over me as her shadow grew smaller, eventually disappearing into the night. I loved the way my heart raced when she was near me, but I knew the day was coming where she would turn and walk away again. She'd head back to the city to live her life and that would be our final goodbye.

25

Addie

The sun was sprawled across my bed the morning everyone would be picking up their gingerbread cookie orders. I rolled toward the window and the brightness caught my eyes. I could feel the soreness in my shoulders from the constant rolling of dough as I pulled the pillow over my face. I needed five more minutes, but both the sun and Hudson weren't going to let that happen. His little paws were kneading the loose strands of my hair that separated the two of us. I pulled the pillow from my face to see his wide eyes.

"I know, I know," I said. "It's time to get up."

I wanted to help my mom set up for breakfast before I headed to the coffeehouse. Trent's mother was arriving today, and Victoria wanted to do a little extra deep clean of their house. I told her that Mom and I could handle it here at the B&B. I counted to three and rolled myself off the bed. Hudson followed me out to the sunroom, and I opened the door to the fenced-in yard to let him outside. I couldn't help but smile at his love for snow. His pink tongue hung out the side of his mouth as he struggled to stay on top of it. I had to call his name at least a dozen times before he decided it was time for him to come back inside.

"Alright, let's go set up the dining room." I pretended he understood as he galloped behind me.

"Good morning sunshine," Mom said. I was just in time. She had a stack of plates in her hand. "Can you grab the glasses and start pouring the water and orange juice?"

"Sure thing," I said. I made a sharp turn into the kitchen and grabbed the tray with everything on it. Hudson bit my heels all the way to the dining room and wasn't much help when I started to set each place for the guests. He grabbed hold of the end of one of the white tablecloths and began to snarl. "Hudson, no!" I kept it at a whisper but tried to be stern. In typical Hudson fashion, he ignored me. Thankfully, he wasn't strong enough to yank it from the table. It kept him occupied while I poured the juice in the glasses, but as soon as I was done, I bribed him with a treat back to my room where he laid on my bed until breakfast was over.

I helped clear everything and threw the last of the dishes into the sink. We had a full house that morning and the dishes were piled up high. I remembered the days in high school when I used to cringe at when it was my turn to wash the dishes after a day like today, but as I scrubbed the hardened pancake batter from the griddle, I smiled. I loved that the B&B was still as popular as ever. The books were full for the next few weeks and the noise that echoed through the halls at each meal was another reminder of what my parent's love had built. I thought about the long journey that got us here as I placed a few more dishes in the drying rack. Then my mom came through the swinging door.

"Shouldn't you be getting ready to head to the coffeehouse?"

"I still have some time," I said. "I can finish these up."

"Nonsense," she said. "Today is a big day for you. I'll finish these."

"Are you sure?" I asked. My arms were elbow deep in foaming soap.

"I'm sure. Go!" She waved me out of the room.

*

Mave was the last person I expected to find when I unlocked the coffeehouse door with Drake's key. I walked in to find her sitting at one of the tables wrapping ribbon around the white boxes. She looked up at me and smiled.

"There's fresh coffee behind the counter."

"Thank you," I said making a beeline for the pot. "I wasn't expecting you this morning."

"I own the place," she said.

"Well, yes, but this was my mess to clean up," I said. I poured the black coffee into the largest mug I could find and carried it back to the table where Mave sat.

Mave pulled out the chair next to her and patted her palm on the seat. I lowered myself into it and took a long sip of my coffee before joining in on finishing up the last of the gingerbread orders.

"You know..." Mave started, "I seem to remember a time back in the day when this coffeehouse needed saving. A tree fell through the roof right there." She pointed to the now covered ceiling tiles above the display counter. "The melted snow seeped in and ruined every bit of the equipment I had. A very generous man came to my rescue. He handled everything while I sulked."

I grabbed the roll of green ribbon that sat in the middle of the table. Once I had a piece the length of my arm, I snipped it with a part of scissors and did the same with the red ribbon. I recalled that same time vividly. After my dad had hired the roofers to fix the gaping hole, he took me and Mave's list of equipment that needed replacing with the check from the insurance company. We spent an hour in the store and stuffed the trunk with all the new equipment. When we got back to the coffeehouse, he hoisted me on the counter while he spent the day putting everything together.

"I remember that day and that man," I said. I tied the ribbon around the top of the white box and got started on the next one.

"I was worried after he was gone that I wouldn't have anyone to save me, but I should've known he wouldn't leave without finding someone to take his place. I can't thank you enough Addie. You helped bring a little light to my Christmas this year."

"I'm glad we could pull it off. Without Drake, I would've been in trouble."

"You like him, don't you?" I was shocked at the boldness of her question. Mave wasn't one to dig deep.

I shrugged, but I couldn't hold in my smile. "I do."

"He's a good one," Mave said. "Guys like Drake are a rare find."

I didn't doubt Mave's words, but the weight of them hit me like a ton of bricks. My time in Cold Spring was running out. I had to be back in the city for the photoshoot in a couple of days and who knew when I'd be back again. After new year came the spring fashion launch and then the summer swim shoot. All of which I would be doing nothing glamorous for. I'd be steaming dresses, holding double-sided tape for the designer, and making dinner reservations. The last few years in the city had diminished the sparkle in my eye when it came to my big dreams, but the few days here in Cold Spring really put a damper on what I thought I was working for in the basement office.

"He is a good one," I said. "It's going to be hard to say goodbye to him."

"I suppose it will."

That was the end of our conversation. A few more swift motions of the hand and all the ribbons were neatly tied onto their boxes. Mave let me handle the rest. She hugged me and disappeared out the front door only moments before the first of the gingerbread cookie customers arrived.

"Hi Millie," I said as her familiar face walked through the door.

"Hello, Miss Addie. What are you doing here?"

"Working," I smiled. "I set up the gingerbread orders on Mave's new website."

"Really? This was such a wonderful idea. I wonder if it would be easy to set up something like that for my flower shop." She tapped her finger against her cheek.

"You absolutely could. It wouldn't be hard at all." I pulled the two boxes that Millie ordered from the pile.

"Do you think you'd be able to help me?" Millie asked.

"Me?" She nodded at the confused look on my face. "Yes! I'd be happy to help."

"Wonderful!" She traded me her business card for the boxes of cookies. "Let me know how much it will cost, and we'll talk after the holidays."

"That sounds great. Merry Christmas Millie." I waved as she headed back out onto Main Street.

I wasn't even at the coffeehouse for an hour before all the orders had been picked up. I had three more business cards in my pile from local stores wanting me to help set them up a new website. All of which were willing to pay me. I had no idea how much to charge, but I was sure planning on looking into it once I got back to the house.

I threw the leftover supplies into a box and walked back around the counter to find an open spot on one of the shelves. I bent down and moved over a few packages of coffee filters and to-go cups and slid the basket neatly in between them right as the bell rang. There were no more orders to pick up, so I figured it was Mave coming back to check on me. I pressed my palms against my thighs and pushed myself back up to find Drake in the middle of the open aisle.

"Hey!" I said. I'm sure he could tell by the way my eyes shot open how surprised I was to see him standing there. So surprised that it took me a minute to realize he wasn't alone.

"Addie, these are my parents. They arrived early. I figured I show them around a bit. Mom, Dad, this is Addie, the girl I was telling you about."

I sauntered out from behind the counter wondering what exactly Drake had told them about me.

"It's so nice to meet you." I raised my hand and his mother reached out first to grab it.

"We've heard such lovely things about you," she said. "I'm glad to see Drake has made himself at home here."

"Drake has been an asset to this town," I said. I slipped my hand from Drake's mom and reached over to his father. "Your son has done wonders for this coffeehouse."

"So I hear." I wasn't fond of the snare in his father's voice and I could tell by the way Drake's hands were heavy in his pockets that he wasn't either.

"You should be proud," I said. "Before Drake, this coffeehouse was nothing but coffee. Most of these tables sat empty. Now, people love coming here for breakfast. My mom owns the B&B up the street and she orders Drake's baked goods every week for our guests."

The only reaction I received from Drake's dad was a nod as he looked around the empty coffeehouse. My words did draw a smile to his mother's face as she wrapped her arm around Drake's shoulder. I hated to run out of there, but the stiffness of the silence in the air was making it hard to breathe.

"I should get back to the house. There's a lot of prepping to do for tomorrow's festivities." I handed Drake the key he'd given me the night before. "I hope you all will come. 'Cookies with Santa' at the Church Street Bed & Breakfast is a popular tradition in this town. We'd love to have you."

"Thanks, Addie." Drake's cheeks flushed as he wrapped his fingers around the key. "We'll sure try."

I nodded and slung my purse over my shoulder. I didn't even bother to bundle up before I opened the door to the cold air. I wrapped my jacket around my shoulders and slipped my hat onto my head as I crossed the street that would lead me home. Poor Drake. My heart was heavy as I walked briskly through town. I hated that at the most magical time of year there was so much hurt in his eyes. After all he'd done for Mave and this town, I couldn't believe his father would find any reason to be disappointed in him.

26

Addie

"Addie, can you grab more milk from the fridge when you're done?" I was slipping on the last piece of my elf costume when my mom yelled down the hallway.

"I will!"

I stood in front of the mirror in my room in a red dress I found in Victoria's closet. It matched the red tights that covered my legs and went perfectly with the green hat on my head. Jennifer let me borrow her black elf shoes to complete the look. I even had a sidekick. In the mirror, I could see Hudson rolling around on the bed as he tried desperately to shake off his reindeer antlers. I reached over and pulled the camera off my dresser to snap some photos of him.

His fluffy brown fur matched the Rudolph look I had in mind perfectly. Even with the limited time I had after everyone picked up the gingerbread cookies, I still was able to snag a red collar with a bell from the General Store to finish up his look. I took a few more photos before I heard my mother yell again.

"Addie!"

"We're coming!" I yelled back. I patted my thighs. "Come on little buddy!"

Christmas Eve was always frantic at the B&B. The guest rooms were full. The usual townies would start ringing the bell any minute and for my mother, everything had to be perfect. It had been that way even before my dad died. She'd oversee the way Victoria and I laid out the cookies, she'd eye me as I mixed the food coloring in the white frosting. Mind you, I've been dying frosting since I was fifteen. This year it looked like Victoria was going to take on that position.

I was heading out of the kitchen with both hands holding a pitcher of milk. I squeezed by her to set them on the table where the milk always goes, at least where it used to go. She was multi-tasking with Dylan wrapped around the front of her with one of those stretchy cloth things.

"Addie!" Victoria snapped. "Those pitchers go on the table with the cookies. She grabbed the pitchers and placed them on each side of a dish with green frosting.

"Since when does the milk go there?" I asked.

"We decided on this last year. People get thirsty while decorating and it causes less traffic and congestion if they have milk right at the decorating table.

That made sense and I knew that Victoria had picked up a lot of the slack since our dad was gone so I didn't want to give her a hard time. I nodded and left it with a *copy that,* before I stepped behind the tripod to get the camera ready. Santa, most fondly known as Frank from the General Store, was already sitting comfortably in his chair. It was almost six o'clock and some of the guests had emerged from their upstairs rooms.

"Good evening Mr. & Mrs. Hemmings," Victoria said. Her voice was much more cordial than when she spoke to me. "Please feel free to grab yourself a glass and a bag of cookies."

Victoria was more than ready for guests to arrive. She had her hand on the door handle before the front bell rang. I watched her from a distance as she twisted the knob and pulled the door open to find Frank's daughter, her husband, and their two sons.

"Merry Christmas Eve! Come on in."

She waved everyone in and guided them to where the line for Santa began. The doorbell rang once again and Victoria did it all over. By six-thirty, Santa had seen more than a dozen kids and the line was still forming. There was no sign of Mave, Drake, or his parents. I texted Drake that morning to make sure he was still coming, but it'd been hours since and I still hadn't received a response.

A few minutes later, when the crowd seemed to quiet down a bit as most of them concentrated on their sugar cookie design, my mother entered the room.

"Hello Everyone! I just wanted to say a quick thank you to all of you for coming," she said. Her hands were raised so people could see where her voice was coming from. "I have been so blessed every year to be able to share this special day with all of you and I am thankful each year that we add new friends to this tradition." She pointed at all the B&B guests that were first-time visitors. "Owning a bed and breakfast was always a dream of mine. I'm so happy that my husband and I were able to make that dream a reality. Every year is special in a unique way. Thank you again for being here. There is plenty of milk and cookies to go around, so don't be shy!"

"Woo hoo!" Victoria clapped and everyone cheered.

I looked down at a young girl in blonde pigtails. She was staying with us this week and I could tell by the way she curled her fingers in front of her mouth that she was afraid of the jolly man in the red suit. She reminded me of myself when I was younger. I bent down to her level and scooped up Hudson who never left my side. I lifted his tiny snout to my ear.

"What's that Rudolph?" I asked. "You have a special request for Santa too? What is it?" I pretended Hudson's extensive kisses were his whisper. "Okay, I'll see what I can do."

I tucked Hudson under my arm and reached my hand out to the young girl.

"I'm Addie the elf. What's your name?"

"Molly," the little girl whispered. Her hands was still covering her face.

"Well, Molly, my little sidekick Rudolph was wondering if you'd want to take a picture with him and Santa."

I think Hudson's kisses on her hands were what convinced her, but I like to think it was my own brilliant idea of making Hudson a reindeer tonight. She pulled her hands from her mouth and started petting Hudson's head. Almost immediately, she nodded and began walking over. Santa took Hudson from my arms, and Molly stepped right up. I went back to the camera.

"Molly, can you tell Santa what you want for Christmas?" I asked. She leaned into his ear, and I leaned down to center the camera before I snapped a few shots. When she was done, I asked her to look over and I captured the big smile that was now on her face. "Good job Molly. It's time for you to go make your cookies."

"Thank you so much," Molly's mom said. "I was expecting to have to be up there with her again this year, but she did great."

"It's my pleasure," I said.

At seven on the dot, Santa's job was done. It was time for him to head out to start delivering presents to the children of the world. With a big HO HO HO, he waved goodbye and reminded the children to make sure they went to bed when their parents told them to tonight. They all nodded their heads and watched Santa's every move until he was out the door.

A few minutes later, the door flew open again. "I think I just saw Santa ride away on his sleigh!" Everyone looked over to see Mave standing at the front door with a long red coat wrapped around her.

"Sorry we're late," Mave said.

Before anyone could ask who she meant by *we*, Drake stepped through the door. Victoria looked over at me from the other side of the room. Her smile was faint, but her eyes were almost bugging out of their sockets. She tilted her head over in Drake's direction. I understood.

"Excuse me," I said. I dabbed my mouth with my napkin and tossed it into the garbage. After one big breath, I walked over to greet the last of the guests.

"Merry Christmas Eve everyone," I said. I took Mave's coat from her hand. "We've got plenty of cookies to decorate, but I understand if you prefer to just enjoy the milk. My hands are still hurting for all that gingerbread making."

Mave laughed. "Thank you, darling. Drake, why don't you help Addie with the coats." Her wink was anything but subtle.

"Will do Mave," Drake stepped toward me, leaving an opening at the front door that his parents soon filled. "Addie, you remember my parents."

"Yes. It's nice to see you again. I'm so glad you could make it."

"It was very nice for you to invite us," Drake's mother smiled. "It seems our son fancy's a bit more in this town than just the bakery."

"Mom!" Drake snapped.

"What?" She shrugged and handed him her white coat. "There's no use in hiding it."

"Come with me," I said and turned down the hall to the coat closet. "How's everything going?" I pulled a hanger from the rack and draped Mave's coat around it.

"Honestly, much better than expected. Everyone we've run into went on and on about me and what I've done for the coffeehouse. At dinner last night, my dad even said something to me he hasn't said since middle school. 'I'm proud of you, son.' I couldn't believe it."

"That's awesome!" I said.

"Anyway, enough about me. Mave told me you were lining up customers yesterday for your new web design company." He winked.

Did I have a web design company? Technically, no, I didn't, but with the slew of business I built up yesterday, maybe it was time to think about starting one. I could use the extra income.

"Millie was so impressed with the new website that when she came to pick up her cookies, she asked if I could help make one for the flower shop. I'm going to go in after Christmas and take some photos and put it all together once I get back to the city," I said.

"Seriously? Good for you!" Drake said.

"She's even going to pay me."

"See, I knew you were wasting your talents in that big city office."

"Yeah yeah." I gave Drake a playful shove. "Hey, Drake..."

"Yeah?"

"Thank you. You did so much for me this past week by setting up the photoshoot and helping me pull off these cookie orders. I thought it was going to be hard coming home this year, but you made it pretty easy."

Drake took my hand in his. With a slight tug, I stepped closer to him. "I feel like I'm the one that should be thanking you. You helped me save Mave's. We made enough money to pay what we owed on the back rent and convinced Mave to open up the online ordering. She's even convinced we should do special orders for Valentine's Day. With part-time help for me in the kitchen. You know, since you won't be here."

I had been trying not to think about the fact that in a couple of days, I'd be leaving. I could see it in the way the corners of Drake's eyes dropped that he was thinking the same thing.

"I'm going to miss you," he said.

"I'm going to miss you too."

Drake swept the palm of his hand across my cheek, and I leaned into it. I lifted my gaze to him. His lips were moving closer to me. I closed my eyes and let his lips press gently into mine. Every time he'd done that, I forgot how to breathe. I held my breath as his lips rested there and wished we could stay like that forever, but our forever was short-lived when Victoria called out from the dining room.

"Hey love birds, sorry to break this up, but I need to squeeze by you. We've got a messy diaper in the house."

I pulled my lips from his. He rested his forehead against mine, and both of us laughed. There wasn't any use in hiding it now. Drake folded his fingers through mine and I held onto him tightly. We might not have had all the time in the world, but we had Christmas, and no matter what happened after I left, that was something I would never forget. We'll always have this Christmas. This was the Christmas that I came back home. It was the Christmas that saved the coffeehouse, and the Christmas my family was put back together again. This Christmas I learned how to deal with loss, how to love, and how to find the magic once again in my small hometown of Cold Spring.

Epilogue

Hudson and I were standing on the train platform waiting for the doors to open. There we were, one year later, heading up to Cold Spring for another Christmas. This year I didn't have to worry about decorating any cookies. The special orders had become so popular that Mave decided to open up the ordering year-round. People were coming from all over to pick up holiday orders that Mave decided to start shipping cookies. First, it was anywhere in the state and now Mave's ships all along the east coast.

Gingerbread cookies are no longer only a Christmas tradition. The orders were coming in so quickly that Mave had to hire additional bakers and she even had to rent out another building down the street to store and ship all the orders. There were gingerbread cookies for Valentine's Day, weddings, baby showers, and more. I remember the day that Mave got the keys to the new building. Drake, her, and I stepped inside.

She looked over at us and said, "figures, all it took was a website."

We all laughed. I through my arm around her and said, "hmm, who would've thought?"

I pained at her elbow in my side but smiled when I looked over at Drake. He gave me a wink.

Speaking of Drake. He still works his magic in the kitchen, but not as much as he used to. He's been busy overseeing his staff and making sure the orders go out on time.

Me? Well, let's just say, this is the last time I'll need to hop a train to Cold Spring for Christmas. I handed in my keys to my New York City apartment a few hours ago and I'm now lugging everything I own back with me via Metro North Railroad.

After finishing up Millie's Flower Shop website, I received a few more calls from local businesses to help them too. I decided to launch a little web design and content development company. As soon as I set up my website, the clients started rolling in. I have clients in Cold Spring, Rhinebeck, Kingston, and all over the Hudson Valley. My camera is no longer collecting dust and I only take orders from myself.

Drake and I signed the papers to our first place together about a month ago. We figured after a year of taking the train every other weekend, it was time to make it official. Most of my clients are in upstate and I had been homesick ever since last Christmas, so it only made sense that if someone had to move, it should be me.

I never thought I would lay down permanent roots in Cold Spring. That's the funny thing about small towns. You spend your whole life trying to escape them. You long for the bright lights and the big city. When you finally break free, one day it hits you. Everything you need. Everything you thought you were running away from; those are the things that matter the most. And once the rebel in you gets it all out of your system, you learn that the one place you belong is home to the one place you wish you'd never left.

...

THE END

Did you love Drake and Addie's story? I sure hope so! If you did, share the love by leaving a review over on Amazon and Goodreads!

ACKNOWLEDGEMENTS

I've always wanted to write a holiday romance! I don't think I could've led with a better first Christmas love story. To my Coffee Queens, you know who you are. Thank you for your endless support and for always lending advice when I needed it. Sara, you were my saving grace on this one. Knowing that you loved this book and were so drawn into it, settled my nerves before I hit the publish button. I wanted it to be perfect and your thoughts helped make it exactly the story it was meant to be.

As always, to my family and friends who continue to share my work and support this crazy dream, I love you all! To my husband, I can't believe I can say that now, I love you for never letting me give up and for pushing me to be a better writer every day.

Can't wait to read more from Courtney Giardina? Here's a sneak peek of her romantic comedy, <u>Falling in London</u>!

1

London's spring weather was not working in Tate Montgomery's favor that morning when she sailed out of her second-story flat. The wind pushed hard against her mid-length black skirt. She could feel the weight on her legs as the heels of her stilettos ferociously hit the cobblestone street. Swarms of people closed in while Tate ruffled through the papers in her hands.

"Don't forget to tell them about the party favors or the music. I love the music."

"I won't forget," Tate muffled into the phone nestled tightly against her shoulder. Genevieve may be more nervous for today than Tate was. She tried to ignore the stutter in Genevieve's voice while fumbling to organize the sheets of paper she'd hastily grabbed off her kitchen counter, but the wind was too strong.

"Crap!" Tate yelled. A single sheet flew from her grasp.

"Are you all right?" Genevieve asked.

Tate didn't answer. Her eyes were locked on the floating paper that had now conveniently wrapped itself around the ankle of a woman walking by. With the risk of breaking an ankle, she lunged over and snatched it.

"Excuse me!" the woman grunted. She glared down at Tate with pursed lips.

"I'm so sorry!" Tate yelled as she struggled to sprint away in her heels. There wasn't time to absorb the judgment falling upon her. Today was a big day, and if she was late, it would ruin it all.

"Tate? Tate, what happened?" Genevieve nudged.

"Nothing. I'm all right now."

Genevieve let out a sigh of relief and dove back into her list of "don't forgets." "The string lights too—be sure to mention those."

"I've got it all ingrained in my head, Genevieve. I won't forget, but I won't even get a chance if I miss this bus."

If it wasn't for hitting the snooze button that morning...twice, Tate would've had eighteen extra minutes. When preparing for the meeting that could make or break a career, those eighteen minutes, she now realized, were everything. It probably would've been fine if Tate ended up wearing the outfit she originally picked out the night before, but, once she had it on, she didn't think it spoke the right words. Not for her first big meeting as CEO of Simple Charms Events. Thank goodness she ended up buying more than one outfit for today. She was also thankful, after changing out of choice number one, that she left the tags on both. If she had worn the first one and forgone the overanalysis in front of her bedroom mirror, her hair might still be in that neatly pulled-back bun she left the house with. Now, she was blinded by the wisps of hair dangling in front of her face. The wind was exceptionally frigid for a spring morning. So much so that Tate's cheeks burned from the bouts of sprinting she was doing.

"Okay, good luck!" Genevieve yelled through the phone. "And don't forget about the art collections."

Tate shook her head. She knew Genevieve couldn't see her through the phone, yet she couldn't help but laugh. "I won't forget about the art collection, I promise. I'll call you later."

Tate shoved the phone back into her purse before Genevieve even had a chance to respond. The bus stop was straight ahead, and she could see the bus right up the street. Morning traffic was working in Tate's favor. The bus inched slowly toward her as she took the last few bounding steps to the sign where it would eventually come to a stop. There was barely enough time to catch her breath before the air brakes burst out in front of her. She pressed her hands quickly against her skirt before the gust of wind revealed what was underneath and then stepped onto the platform.

Her bobby pins had let her down. Tate could now see just how many strands of hair were flying free around her face in the reflection of the bus window as she squeezed her way into an empty seat on the lower deck. Her shoulder rubbed against the man next to her as she attempted to remove her compact out of the front pocket of her laptop bag. There wasn't much wiggle room between the rotund man sitting in the window seat and those standing in the aisle on her other side.

You'd think by now Tate would've mastered this public transport thing. She never drove anymore, but she also was lucky enough to not have to regularly ride during rush hour. It was 9:00 a.m., prime time for the London workforce, which meant for the next few stops she'd be crammed in like a sardine. Her fingertips pressed hard against the compact as she slid it out of the pocket of her laptop case. To get a good look, Tate squeezed the compact between her knees and readjusted a few of those bobby pins in order to hide the disheveled parts of her hair. A few dabs of powder hid the bright red cheeks brought on by the London air, and, for the remaining stops, she closed her eyes and went over her big presentation in her mind.

Tate's eyes blinked open right as the Westminster Cathedral came into view. That meant her stop was next. She reached for the handle above and pulled herself up to stand while eyeing the stunning piece of architecture that dazzled Victoria Street. Westminster Cathedral was not to be confused with Westminster Abbey. That was one of the first things Tate learned when she moved to London. Prince William did not get married at the Westminster Cathedral, and if you messed that up, the locals, understandably so, would be sure to fire their wrath of disapproval for not taking the time to research the details of their beloved city.

"Excuse me." Tate tapped the shoulder of a dapper man with pepper hair who was blocking the aisle beside her. He turned to look over his shoulder.

"Could I squeeze by you?" she asked.

He nodded and stepped aside. As the bus slowed, Tate took a few more steps forward, excusing herself until she reached the front platform. When the doors opened, she stepped down into another rush of business suits. That same brisk air hit her again, and her arms tingled. It was a crisp ten degrees across the city today—Celsius, that is. In translation, that was about fifty degrees Fahrenheit. Though not the coldest Tate had experienced since her move to London, her west coast roots were still adjusting to fifty degrees in April. Today was typical of what winter months had looked like growing up in Seattle, but by now, it most likely would be nearing the seventies back home. Tate knew she had another month or so of days like this left here in London before the seventies arrived, but she embraced the cold weather. Cold weather meant a few more months of hot coffee. That was her favorite combination and the first thought in her mind as the bus pulled away.

Tate didn't have time to take in the beauty of the redbrick scaling the nineteenth-century stature of the Westminster Cathedral. She clasped her coat tighter as the wind pushed back. Brick buildings surrounded her as her legs fought through the dense air. Her laptop bag swung heavily at her side, and her heels clicked beneath her as she thought about how she got here.

Two years ago, when she first came to London, she had been lucky enough to land an assistant job with one of the most influential event planning agencies in the city. Rosewood Events was known for hosting some of the most extravagant parties for London's elite. With a degree in hospitality management, it seemed like a logical next step for the girl whose long-anticipated future plans had changed suddenly. The dozens of weddings, galas, and charity functions were a welcome distraction for more than a year. After that, though, Tate decided to step out on her own.

Over the past six months, she'd planned a few small parties and company events. The foundation for Simple Charms was steadily being built. Genevieve, her best—and right now, only—friend in London, had agreed to be her very first employee. Tate still didn't believe that when she said it out loud. She had an *employee*. Someone she actually paid to work for her. Not only that, she was growing so fast, she'd reached out to a local university for internships. More hands meant more events, and Tate was happy with how her event planning baby was growing, but this... This could be the event that would send her career soaring. If she booked this, she could afford to hire more employees and take on even more events.

She needed to nail this presentation.

"Oh, thank you!" Tate smiled. She reached out for the door of the coffee shop being held open by a young woman. The aroma of coffee was abundant as Tate stepped inside. Primrose May had become Tate's favorite meeting spot. She didn't even mind that she passed up a dozen other places between her flat and this quaint corner shop; she loved the ambiance here. The white brick walls were painted with inspirational quotes and floral murals. Long bar tables lined each side of the entry along the floor to ceiling windows, and the solid white chairs and wood tables left an opening down the middle of the room, where only a few people stood in line in front of her.

The clock was ticking, but Tate couldn't show up to this meeting without her coffee order. When Tate first started Simple Charms events, she knew standing out would be hard. There were dozens of big-name companies like Rosewood in the area. Her resume wasn't quite as impressive...yet, so she focused on the one skill she did have: hospitality. There wasn't anything anyone loved more in the morning than a nice warm cup of coffee. It took a little research on Tate's part, but she succeeded every time at finding out her clients' favorite type of drink. She'd walk into the meeting, hand it over, and watch the smile grow on her potential client's face. It was her special little touch, and that morning wasn't any different. The only thing out of the ordinary was the new face at the counter.

"Are you okay?" the young girl asked once Tate was at the register.

"I am, thank you."

That question was something Tate had spent a long time getting used to when she first moved here. Every time someone asked her if she was okay, she'd look down wondering what was wrong with her. Did she have mascara under her eyes? Was she bleeding from somewhere? She learned quickly that "Are you okay?" in London meant the same as "How are you?" or "Can I help you?" did back in America. Even now she knew, it wouldn't stop her from looking at her reflection on the way out just to make sure.

"I'll have a half-caff and an Americano, both medium, to go, please." Tate smiled.

"Anything else?"

"I think that's it." She handed over her credit card. "Are you new here?"

The girl slid the credit card into the slot in front of her. "Yes. I started last week."

Tate's eyes squinted to read the name tag secured over the girl's black shirt. One of the reasons she loved Primrose May so much was that everyone there knew her name, and she knew theirs. Now, there was one more to add to her list.

"Well, it's nice to meet you, Isla. I'm Tate."

Isla pulled Tate's card out of the slot and handed it back to her. "It's nice to meet you too." Her cheeks flushed as she rested the card in Tate's open palm.

Tate was thankful for the momentary distraction, but once she stuffed her card back into her wallet, the nerves returned. The vibration was heavy in her hands as she leaned against the counter at the back waiting for her name to be called. The coffee shop was lively with conversation, which, for a moment, distracted her. Two women about her age stared intently at one of their cell phones. Their bellow of laughter almost overpowered Isla when she called Tate over for her order. Luckily, Tate caught her out of the corner of her eye as she slid two cups of coffee onto the bar. Tate's hands were still slightly shaking, but she managed to get a firm grip on both before she jetted back out of the door onto the busy London street.

With only a few minutes to spare, Tate clutched both cups tightly in her hands and walked up the steps to the hotel for her meeting. She stretched out her pinkie as far as it would reach for the handle on the door. This was it. The beat of her heart was now rapidly pounding like a drum solo in her chest. She was only a few steps away from the moment she had been preparing for day in and day out this past week. That door was the only thing standing between her and what would hopefully be victory.

At least, she thought that door was the only thing.

Just as her pinkie was about to wrap around the handle, the door flew open from the inside. A man stepped out onto the steps and right into Tate's path. It didn't end there. She stumbled backward and lost her grip on one of the to-go cups. A stream of coffee was now flying through the air.

The cup bounced a couple of times before eventually coming to a rolling stop on the ground. Half of what was inside had ended up on the ground with it, while the other half was soaking into the front of Tate's brand-new blouse.

"I am so sorry," Tate heard a voice say once the shock wore off.

The peacoat she was wearing was buttoned just low enough that the coffee had missed it completely, but her blouse, the one she chose specifically to show off at this meeting, had taken the brunt of this unfortunate event.

"Here, let me help you." The man in the suit reached for her hand, but Tate brushed it off. She was too busy assessing the tie-dyed look of her blouse.

"Are you kidding me?" she screamed shaking off the coffee on her hands. "Don't you watch where you're going?"

"I'm really sorry," he said. "I didn't see you there."

Tate looked up at him for the first time. His golden hair was unfazed by the gust of wind that suddenly swept between them. Underneath his gray jacket was an ocean blue tie that seemed only a shade darker than the blue in his eyes. She could see the pained expression on his face, but in that moment, she didn't really care. He would walk out of the hotel as clean and put together as he had walked in, and she was cringing at the wetness of the permanent stain she could feel seeping through her silky white button-up.

"Excuse me," he yelled to the front desk "could you get me some napkins?" He looked back at Tate. "Let me help you."

The man bent down to pick up the empty cup, which, thankfully, ended up being Tate's beloved Americano. The half-caff she'd ordered for her client was still safely in her left hand. The concierge showed up with a handful of napkins, which Tate snatched from him. Her nose scrunched as she patted herself down.

"I think you've done enough," Tate said.

"No, really, at least let me dry-clean it or something. Here, give me your number, and I'll..."

"Seriously?" she snarled and glared at him. "You're asking for my number?"

"No, I didn't mean... I just want to help."

She watched the corner of his eyelids droop and, for a second, thought about accepting his apology. That moment quickly faded as the strike of a clock echoed from the nearby church.

"I'm going to be late!" she panicked.

"Wait—please!" he yelled.

"Sorry, I've got to go." She pushed past him and sprinted into the hotel lobby.

Tate ran to the nearest bathroom to inspect the damage. The coffee hadn't made its way to the white tank top she wore underneath the blouse. She pulled off her coat, unbuttoned the blouse, and shoved it into her bag, then looked in the mirror again and hiked the tank top up a bit higher to hide the lace of her bra before putting her peacoat back on. She fluffed up her coat a little, hoping it would erase the mayhem that ensued at the front door. So much for the CEO outfit she had so gracefully pieced together. She was going to have to present her vision in a full-length brown coat.

Tate looked down at the zebra stripes covering her feet. *At least my heels are cute.* Those were her final thoughts before she pushed through the bathroom door and into the lion's den.

Grab your copy of Falling in London now to see what happens next!

About Courtney

I am a firm believer that we should never go a day without living our passions.

That's why the characters in my novels become your best friends and you turn the final pages of my books feeling empowered, overly caffeinated and on the search for your next adventure.

I grew up just outside of Rochester, NY where I have always had a lively imagination and a reach for the stars attitude.

When I was younger, I wanted to be a pirate. Yes, you read that right. My family used to spend their summers vacationing in the Thousand Islands where each year the town held a Pirate's Weekend. That's where my love of pirates began.

I also loved cheerleading and gymnastics. When my dreams of being a pirate and Olympic gymnast fell through, I turned to another love...writing.

As a creative, I have not only published multiple novels, but have appeared on TV shows like *Nashville*. If I can do anything in life, I hope to inspire others to dream big and believe in themselves because life is too short to wonder, "what if."

Learn more about Courtney at www.courtneygiardina.com

Made in the USA
Columbia, SC
28 November 2020